MONTANA SKY

Montana, book 6

RJ SCOTT

Love Lane Books

Montana Sky

Montana series, book 6

Copyright ©2019 RJ Scott

Cover design by Meredith Russell, Edited by Sue Laybourn

Published by Love Lane Books Limited

ISBN 9781095643075

All Rights Reserved

Dedication

For everyone who wanted to know what happened to the man that Justin let live.
Thank you to LeeAnn for the rings :)

And, always for my family.

RJ SCOTT

Montana 6

MONTANA
Sky

Chapter One

MARTIN BRIEFLY STOPPED ON THE STONE BRIDGE AND tipped his head to the sky. The rain had finally stopped, and stars dotted the vast black canvas untainted by light pollution. He was here, and he'd never felt so at a loss of what to do next.

Crooked Tree Ranch. Justin and Adam.

Why did I think it was a good idea to come to Montana?

Moonlight illuminated tiny parts of the darkness that shrouded Crooked Tree, and he turned full circle. There was only enough light to hint at the shape of things; a road that ended in the parking lot, a restaurant, reflective signs indicating where areas of the ranch lay from this central point. This way was admin, next to it, Branches Restaurant, and behind him was a notice about the distance to the cabins on foot, cycle, and by horse.

Below the bridge, the river rushed over large boulders and the noise mesmerized him long enough that he temporarily forgot the dread gripping his chest. Then it crashed back down on him and he questioned why was he standing there as if he had all the time in the world.

I need to know why Justin didn't kill me. Then I can leave.

"I got your message."

Martin jumped at the voice coming from the dark. *Justin.*

"Shit, you scared me."

Justin stepped out of the shadows. "When I gave you that number it was for you to call me, not ask to come here. What do you want, Jamie?"

"I'm not Jamie," Martin corrected immediately. "My name is Martin. Martin Graves. You know that; you know I can't use Jamie anymore."

I don't want to use that name.

Justin leaned against the facing wall, arms crossed over his chest. Although his stance was intimidating, his expression was neutral; most importantly he didn't look as if he was going to kill Martin. Even though three years ago in the coffee shop, Justin had unconditionally promised Martin he was safe from Justin killing him, it remained one of the more persistent fears chasing him in his nightmares. Martin lowered his hands, slowly, and willed his heart to start beating because his chest felt tight, and he was convinced he was about to drop dead.

That would mess everything up.

"I need to talk to you," Martin answered, pushing his hands into his pockets and nudging his dropped bag back against the wall. "I need to know why you let me live."

"What?"

This wasn't going well. Martin didn't exactly want anything rational, and Justin hadn't moved, only stared at him as if he expected a grand speech. Martin did have a speech planned. Hell, he'd considered very carefully what he was going to say. In some scenarios, he spoke impassioned words, talking about what his dad had done, what he'd become, how his dad had hurt Justin and Adam, and how Martin carried that with him every day. How sorry he was. How his whole life in Vermont had gone up in flames and he needed somewhere to stop. In others, he told Justin that he'd found peace, held back the demons, and learned to live with the nightmares.

"You could have shot me, left me for dead, finished the kill list you had, but you didn't. Why?"

"Hell if I know," Justin said.

Martin took an instinctive step backward, his thighs hitting the wall. Justin left a foot between them, and waited.

"Was it because you saw something in me?" Martin asked desperately.

"Nope," Justin said.

Martin's heart sank. "But, when you said you wouldn't kill me, you told me to find you one day and tell you that I knew I was brave. Did you think I was brave? Really? Is that why you didn't kill me?"

"You can't stay." Justin glanced over his shoulder toward the restaurant as if he didn't want to be seen on this bridge talking to a stranger.

"Answer my question," Martin demanded. He'd come here straight from his mom's funeral, hitchhiked his way to Helena, used the last of his money on a bus, walked the last four hours in a rain that had only let up for short amounts of time. Exhausted and soaked to the bone, his carefully constructed life was unraveling, and he needed this to stop.

"You should be anywhere but here," Justin said. "If anyone sees you and tells Adam, it could hurt him."

"God, is Adam here?" The last thing that Martin wanted was to see Adam. It was enough that he had approached Justin right now.

"No." Justin let out an impatient sigh. "You need to leave."

Martin couldn't leave, he needed an answer.

"I'm not brave. You said I was brave, but was that the only reason you didn't kill me? I have nothing else to hold on to when I don't believe I am brave at all." He shivered not just from the cold but from the icy feel of a hundred ghosts crawling under his skin. The rain started again, and Martin pushed his hair away from his face and was utterly lost.

They stood in silence for a while; then Justin cursed noisily. "Fuck. Let's get the hell out of this rain."

Justin headed up the hill, and after a pause, Martin followed. The restaurant building was internally lit with security lights, but they weren't a glaring white, more of a subtle yellow gold in the rain. It was made of wood, sprawling into the trees, clear glass showcasing a gorgeous interior with more wood, and a counter toward the back.

"In here," he said and opened the door to let Martin through. The warmth inside made his skin prickle, and he immediately shrugged off his soaked coat. Being warm and dry was a luxury, and he'd take it over cold and wet any day.

Justin checked him up and down. "Jesus kid, you look like shit. When did you last eat?"

Martin wanted to point out that Justin was only a year older than him and that *kid* wasn't a good description, but he didn't. All he could think about was the last time he'd had a proper meal, which had to be five or six days ago. He'd filled up on cheap gas station snacks, but a hot meal with real food, that was a distant memory. He knew he'd lost a bit of weight when his jeans found a new natural level resting on his hips.

"Not today," he evaded.

Justin ushered him to a table and then went to the counter, talking to a shorter man Martin hadn't even noticed was there. The second man leaned sideways to glance around Justin— right at Martin, and he frowned. The two of them exchanged heated words before the other man gave a full-body sigh and disappeared. Justin came back, turning the chair at the table to straddle it.

He was probably waiting for Martin to say something smart or insightful to explain what the hell he was doing here. They stared at each other in silence.

"Why didn't you kill me?" Martin asked, again.

"Tell me what happened in Vermont," Justin changed the subject immediately. "I know you have no job, that the place you worked at burned to the ground under suspicious circumstances."

"How did you know that?"

Justin shook his head and huffed. "You really think I left you there without checking on you?" Then he leaned closer and his expression was hard. "I had to be sure you weren't really your father's son."

That cut deep. Even after fighting as hard as he had against his birthright, he was David Crane's son after all. *Bad blood runs in my veins.* One small push and his father's legacy of evil could emerge and crack him wide open. Temper would make him hurt people, and fear would drive him to destroy everything that was right.

His heart hurt, and he stood slowly. Three years since Justin had spared his life, and in all that time, Martin had held on to the fact that someone had actually appeared to care about him. Justin was the one person he thought might understand or at least show something akin to compassion, but he'd been wrong. *Who can blame him, after what I was part of?*

"I understand." He slammed a lid on the acidic self-hatred that boiled up inside. "I'll go now."

"Fuck's sake, kid, sit down."

Martin instantly reacted to the forcefulness of Justin's tone. He'd grown up used to people telling him when to sit or stand or hurt people, another part of his messed-up psyche he had no control over. He sat, carefully, every muscle in his body aching.

"I'm not a kid," he said. "I'm only a year younger than you are."

Justin ignored him, went to fetch a water jug and glasses, and retook his seat. Carefully he poured out a glass and nudged it toward Martin.

"Tell me about the fire," he said. "Start at the beginning."

Clearly Justin wasn't going to answer Martin's question, and what else could Martin do but sit and talk? It was raining, he was only just warming up, there was coffee, and he didn't want to leave yet.

"Everything was razed to the ground. We have a lot of contractors near there, buildings going up, and we were the last place left that wouldn't sell to them. I don't know if I can point at them as being responsible, but they knew the owner wasn't interested in selling." He couldn't meet Justin's gaze. "I didn't start the fire."

Justin studied him thoughtfully, then nodded. "Of

course you didn't. I know that."

Martin wanted to take that as a win, that small good thing that Justin had offered him, but his thoughts were chaotic.

"Wait? Were you watching that as well?" Martin wouldn't put anything past the enigmatic Justin with his ninja assassin skills and his ability to track Martin down all those years ago, despite how hard Martin had tried to hide. "Or are you saying you don't think I could do it."

Justin looked thoughtful.

"Just because your father was a domestic terrorist consumed with hate, and you were part of it when you were younger, it doesn't mean you're one of the bad guys now."

Martin glanced around him, wishing Justin wasn't talking so loudly. The connection to his dad was something he never talked about, and even though the restaurant was closed and empty except for the three of them, he didn't want the words out there.

"I was never part of it, not really. I was trapped there as much as you were," Martin defended.

Justin stared at him steadily, and Martin met the stare.

"Not quite the same way," he murmured. "You had the freedom to run."

"You think I didn't try that? I was terrified." *Why am I defending myself? Justin doesn't care. Hell, I don't freaking care.*

Justin had every reason to expect Martin to have done every evil thing his blood made him capable of. Including burning down the café.

"Well, right now I have no reason to doubt you. Of course, that could change."

Justin sipped water and watched Martin over the rim

of his glass, his expression focused and thoughtful.

Martin cleared his throat. "I'd been working hard at the café, community outreach, that kind of thing. Not that there was much of a community left after the big corporations bought up the old houses to replace them with trendy apartments." His words ran together. "When the café burned down, Joe didn't want to rebuild. So I had no job, or a place to live because I'd been sleeping in my room above the café. I needed to talk to you, to understand what you saw in me, and then I'm heading south."

"South? Texas? Florida? Mexico?"

"The ocean," Martin said, and that was about all he had to tell right now. To him, the ocean was as vast as the sky, and he wanted to lie on a beach and stare up at the blue and hear the wash of waves as he decided what to do next with his life.

Coffee arrived then. The shorter guy seemed as if he was weighed down by the thundercloud of anger buzzing around his head. Both coffees met the table forcefully, liquid sloshing over the mugs. Martin thought he was watching some kind of comedy double act. Justin looking chagrined; the short guy pissed.

"This is my partner, Sam," Justin said. *He knows who you are; he knows everything* remained unspoken.

Martin held out his hand for Sam. "Hi."

Sam ignored his overture and instead stared at him with narrowed eyes.

"So you're *him*." His tone was flat. "Jamie."

"This is *Martin*," Justin inserted with emphasis, and Sam shot him a heated stare.

The last thing he wanted was a debate about his real name and why he wasn't using it. As far as he was concerned, Jamie Crane had died the same day Justin and Adam had been hurt.

He flushed and stared down at the menu on the table. For a brief hopeful moment Sam appeared to be leaving, and then at the last moment, he turned back and took one of the chairs at their table. He leaned in and pushed at Martin's arm to make him look up.

"If you drag Justin back to anything, I will hurt you, okay?" He kept his tone low, but there was so much anger dripping from the words that Martin moved back in his chair and looked for the exit.

"Sam, it's okay," Justin said, sounding tired, then covering Sam's hand with his own. "Nothing he brings with him will hurt me, no memories or experiences or people. Okay?"

"But what about Adam? What about him?"

Justin shook his head mutely.

"Promise me," Sam whispered, just loud enough for Martin to hear, and then leaned into Justin and pressed a kiss to his lips.

"I promise."

"And you'll be the one to tell Adam when he and Ethan get back from vacation?"

"I will."

"The day they get back."

"Yep."

At that, Sam straightened and nodded at Martin, although there was no welcoming smile, just a fixed stare that discouraged him. "Then I'll get food."

Only when Sam had gone did Justin lean forward.

"We need to talk about your mom."

And the bottom fell out of Martin's carefully constrained world.

Chapter Two

THE URGE TO RUN WAS STRONG. MARTIN STARED AT THE door, willing himself to stand. Justin most have read his intention and went over and locked it before sitting back down. That had been Martin's last escape route, so now he was stuck. He'd promised to never talk about his mom, and the vow was too fresh to even think of breaking it.

"What about my mom?"

"I know she died."

Martin blanched. No one who mattered was supposed to know about his birth mother. He'd made a promise to her new husband that he'd never mention his connection to Louisa Coleman or to Louisa's daughter, Alice.

My little sister.

It was an easy promise to make; anything to keep Alice safe. He'd seen her at the funeral, the same wavy hair as him, a shade lighter, and her eyes hidden behind dark glasses. She'd leaned on her stepdad and cried as he'd held her. It would have been so easy to walk over and talk to Alice, but he hadn't. He'd been told to leave, by the Senator's security guards, so he'd left. That was where that part of his life story had ended.

He gripped the table so hard his knuckles whitened, then shook his head mutely. Justin waited a moment, making it obvious he was expecting an answer.

"I won't talk about my mom."

"What about your sister?"

"How do you…? Don't you even mention her. I don't want to talk about anything to do with her."

"Does she know what happened back with your dad?"

"I said I won't talk about her." Martin tilted his chin, waiting for Justin to demand he go and tell his only living blood relative everything. Like hell, he would do that.

"Did you go to the funeral? Did you even speak to her?"

"You tell me. After all, you're the one tracking me."

Justin shook his head. "I just know she died, is all."

"It is what it is," Martin said and shrugged for emphasis. He could show the world he didn't care that his mom had died. She'd been gone from his life a long time; he didn't have much memory of her. He'd found her though, through her maiden name. She'd married a politician who was aiming high, became the perfect wife, always in the papers fundraising for this, that, or the other. Of course, he'd set up an alert on his phone to track her, just in case of… something.

Then there was Alice, his sister. She had a beauty blog, with a nice sideline in charitable works, and had just graduated with a degree in Art History. They weren't brother and sister through nurture, but part of his heart would always connect to hers.

Then the men had suggested he leave. Warned him off. Told him in no uncertain terms it was dangerous for him to be there. He'd taken it at the time that somehow he was a danger to his sister, but in hindsight, they'd been saying he'd be in danger if he didn't go.

He'd left quickly. No point in mourning a mom he didn't know, or worrying about a sister who might not even have known he was alive.

"I don't *want* to be here," Martin said after the longest pause, with emotion choking him. *But I have nowhere else to go, and I need help.*

"I know you don't. Let's face it, no one wants you here."

The words cut deep; of course no one wanted him at Crooked Tree, and he could understand why, but Justin had been the only person he thought he wanted to connect with. Even briefly.

"I won't hurt you and Adam."

Justin raised an eyebrow. "You wouldn't get the chance, even if you wanted to." The menacing words struck a chord. He'd never seen Justin in action, but to know that this man had single-handedly taken down his father and probably the rest of his father's fellow domestic terrorists meant he had to be good. The group, his father included, had all been trained in survival and hand-to-hand combat to a level surpassing that of a normal civilian—all good soldiers fighting for their version of the perfect white America.

Sam banged and crashed in the kitchen, and Martin winced.

"I don't want to cause any trouble for you with Sam."

"You won't."

Sam arrived with what looked like breakfast: crispy bacon, pancakes, eggs, hash browns. And this time he placed the plates dramatically on the table. "You look ill," Sam said.

"I'm not ill—"

"Eat."

"Thank you," Martin managed and picked up the gleaming silverware as Sam stalked back to his kitchen. It was midnight now, and he wasn't about to turn down a free meal.

Justin didn't begin to eat, only stared at him as if he could see inside Martin's soul. Justin had a hardness about him that was terrifying, but what did Martin expect? After all, he was responsible for making Justin the man he was today. He'd been part of the group who'd hurt him and Adam.

"Do you sleep?" he asked.

"As well as I can." *Sometimes the nightmares pull me into a terror I don't want to recall, but mostly I can sleep.*

"Nightmares?"

"Some."

"Finish your food, and I'll find you a bed somewhere."

Martin blinked at Justin, not sure he'd heard right. "I don't need a bed. Once you answer my question about what stopped you killing me, then I told you I'm heading south. Thank Sam for the coffee and food, but I need to find somewhere else to stay. I never intended to stay."

Justin took Martin's hand, his hold firm. "I can make you stay, Martin."

Fear gripped Martin, "Are you threatening me?"

Of course he's threatening me. He hates me after what I did to him. This is some kind of revenge—as twisted as what hurt him and Adam. He probably had a gun, as he had when he came to the cafe three years ago

"No," Justin said without hesitation. "I'm saying Crooked Tree is a safe place for you to stop for a while and to take a breath. If you want to leave, then you can go. I won't stop you. And one day soon I might explain why I didn't kill you. Just not now."

All the fire left Martin instantly, and he sat back in his chair as if his strings had been cut.

"Really?"

Justin huffed a laugh and focused on the coffee mug, drawing his finger around the rim. "There's no way to rationalize the horrors we saw or what your father and his *friends* did. Believe me, I tried. But there is a life beyond those ghosts, and you need to rest somewhere, Martin. Just for a while, until Adam comes back, maybe Crooked Tree might just be the right place for you to stop."

Chapter Three

Tyler Colby dropped the last of his bags in the cabin and watched the cab as it reversed into to the parking lot. The driver had waited at the main area of Crooked Tree as Tyler had collected the keys to his place from one of the ranch guys. The total for the cab's time was huge when it appeared on his phone seconds later, right behind the perfectly timed email from his boss.

Elizabeth's message was simple. It contained a copy of the schedule they'd worked up between them, and had an added reminder for him to keep detailed records, including receipts for reimbursement. The word *receipts* was in bold, and Tyler couldn't help but smile. He'd worked in the Earthquake Studies Office for three years now and had never once filed one of those horrendously complicated and needless expense reports with the Montana Bureau of Mines and Geology, much to Elizabeth's horror. She'd pulled him to the side yesterday and scolded him for not following the rules. Yet another set of rules and the part of his job where he couldn't tolerate the bureaucracy. Why bother messing around with dollars and cents, when what they should all be doing was focusing on the cutting edge projects that could save lives?

"Stupid-ass forms," he murmured as he poked into the rooms of Forest Cabin six. It had four huge bedrooms, three of which he would be converting into office space, a decently equipped kitchen, and a small laundry room. A sitting room with comfortable sofas and a TV was in the center of the cabin, with floor-to-ceiling windows and views over a small grass yard that merged into the trees.

Crooked Tree was a stunning place, but it wasn't all about the trees for him or even the river as it rushed through the ranch. The beauty lay underneath his feet as he imagined the washed away sediment, and visualized the layers of time snaking beneath the land, along with the carved patterns left by retreating ice. The ranch was in a prime position for the next seismic tracker to be added to the network and soon to be part of the early warning system for seismic disturbance.

The sitting room was where he would set up boards, start collating information, and begin constructing the newest addition to the Montana Regional Seismic Network. The new installation would be one of the most remote they had, but he'd argued that there was too much territory outside Helena that wasn't being monitored. He'd been proven right in the last 3.5 magnitude, 2 km depth point quake that had rattled windows and opened up new cracks in old ground. Then the higher-ups at the Department began to listen and apply for government grants.

Installing a permanent seismic station here on

Crooked Tree land was a small step in the grand scheme of things, but it was also Tyler's baby, and he was going to do it right.

Last July, there'd been an earthquake south of Lincoln that people had felt from Spokane to Billings, but it had occurred along a fault not previously mapped by the team of seismologists he was part of. That was what had drawn him here because this region was less studied than the seismically active West Coast. He was at this location to examine the recent earthquake swarms in Yellowstone, and he was going to find a way to save lives.

That was his goal and had been since he was fourteen.

He pulled out the parts for the first whiteboard setup —it was the easiest starting point—then he laid everything out as the instructions said he should. He had a PhD. Surely he should be able to assemble flat pack boards and A-frames.

"Dr. Colby?" someone called from the open door, and Tyler waved them in, concentrating on setting up his first board and not quite getting tab A to click into tab B. "I'm here with your supplies. Where do you want them?"

"Kitchen counter," he said, breathing through the mild irritation that this particular inanimate object wasn't bending to his will. *I don't have time for this shit.*

There was a clatter of objects, the rattle of something, and after Tyler finally managed to click the tabs into place, he sought out the source of all the noise. Whoever it was seemed to take great joy in making one hell of a lot of racket, and locating the sound, he found the owner of the sounds crouching in front of one of the base units, juggling cans of food and two jars of sauce. He was in that impossible situation where he couldn't put something down without dropping another of the items he held, and smoothly Tyler reached down to help. Between them, they put everything where it should be, and then the man stood, and Tyler got his first look at him.

He was taller than Tyler by just a couple of inches, curly hair in disarray around his face, and eyes the color of green glass. He wore a uniform of jeans and a sweatshirt emblazoned with a horse logo, and the cap on his head told Tyler that *Horses Are The Best.*

That statement didn't convince him. Rock strata and a moving, angry earth, now *that* was the best.

"Tyler," he extended a hand, which the man took readily.

His handshake was firm, and it didn't last long. "Martin. They said I should put the food away for you. So I didn't want to leave it on the counter."

His words sounded uncertain, the kind of tone that made Tyler feel Martin suspected being sent to do that job was a huge joke being played on him. Or maybe he was nervous about walking into an occupied cabin?

"Thank you, Martin. Don't suppose you want to volunteer to cook all this for me as well." He was teasing. This was banter, but Martin ignored him and took a step back, dropping his gaze to another bag and picking it up to unpack the contents into the double-wide fridge. Tyler pressed on through the awkward silence. "I can't cook to save my life," he deadpanned.

Martin didn't react at all, just lined up eggs in the storage container.

Tyler leaned over and picked up one of them. "I

mean, I like eggs, but I can't do much more than scramble them. I had the best soufflé in Paris once, and the chef tried to show me, but yep, I scrambled the mix when I tried to make one. And I won't even begin to explain what happened in London when I attempted to make egg fried rice. Let's just say the firefighters were hot to look at until they started to laugh at me. Apparently I wasn't the first person to burn up a kitchen, but I was the first who'd done it trying to boil rice without adding water."

Why can't I stop talking?

That was a simple question to answer: because Martin wasn't saying a thing, and there was nothing that Tyler hated more than silence when he was with someone.

"I don't know why I ordered all this stuff," he continued. "No, that's not entirely true. I do know really. I'm here for at least a few weeks, so I decided I wouldn't eat at the restaurant every day. I need to have some form of self-sufficiency, or so people tell me, but I can't live off trail mix as I do when I'm out working, and it's not like I can order in a chef or food."

Martin didn't reply, and Tyler wanted him to talk because the man's voice was smooth, and he had a stoic quietness about him that was intriguing.

"Uh-huh," Martin finally offered, then turned back to what he was doing.

"Have you worked at Crooked Tree a long time?"

"No." Martin shut the fridge door and piled up the bags. "That's all of it." He headed for the door, and Tyler thought that was them finished, but as Martin reached it, he turned. "Please call the office if you want to order anything to restock."

Tyler sent him a cautious smile as Martin shut the door behind him, and then crossed to the window to watch him leave. He was driving a ranch SUV, and Tyler got a look at his profile before he drove away. Very sexy in a quiet curly haired kind of way, with those serious eyes.

"Repeat after me, Tyler. You do not want to lust after indifferent men you don't know."

But Martin was gorgeous, all focused on his job and shy or deferential. Tyler couldn't tell. He just knew the man ticked all his weird-ass boxes, and that was certainly one way to spend the downtime at the ranch. Not that there would be much in the way of downtime or even time at the ranch. He had too much to do, which reminded him.

"Whiteboards."

Chapter Four

MARTIN HAD BECOME A MASTER AT AVOIDING TALKING TO Justin. Or indeed being anywhere in Justin's vicinity. Over the last five days, he'd also become very dedicated at carrying out his job at Crooked Tree: fetching, carrying, restocking the small ranch shop, and delivering grocery orders like the one this morning to the over-talkative but gorgeous guy in Forest Cabin six. He'd helped to bus tables in Branches on two occasions. Sam had made it very obvious that he hadn't wanted him there, but Martin had kept his head down and done his job. Which was exactly what he was doing right now. After managing the Coffee Bean for six years, he'd gotten to the point where he could juggle orders in his sleep.

Noon, and a family of four had taken the table by the window. It was prime real estate, with views of the stone bridge and the river, with the mountains beyond, and had quickly become his favorite table to bus. Any time he got a glimpse of the outside made him happy.

Add in the fact this was his first morning of taking orders, and he felt calm and focused.

The dad took the menu gratefully. "What's good here? We've been driving all night, and I can't even see straight now." He said all of this as he helped his daughter with a shoelace and glanced over at his son, who wanted to show him something on his cell phone. He didn't appear harried or pissed. If anything, he was juggling all the demands like a pro.

"Mom, Dad's not doing it right," the daughter whined. She was tired and on the verge of crying.

Mom took over and hugged her daughter, and Dad looked up at him expectantly. He didn't snap at his daughter or shout at his wife, and his son was drooping.

"How about something quick to eat?" Martin suggested, "Then maybe you can get back to the cabin and get some sleep?" He wanted to bite back the words as soon as he said them. It wasn't his place to comment on whether a guest needed sleep.

But Dad smiled up at him. "That would be great."

"Have you checked in yet?"

Dad shook his head. "Not yet."

"How about meatball subs? We have a vegetarian option. Both of them are seasoned with marjoram and rosemary and simmered in a homemade tomato sauce, and they're possibly the best meatballs I've ever tasted. I can bring over some salads as well?"

"Oh god, that sounds wonderful," Mom said. "Eat, sleep. In that order."

He asked about drinks and handed the entire order to Sam, who, Martin realized, had been staring at him for at least the last part of the transaction at the table.

"Can I ask a question?" Martin was cautious about

asking Sam anything. After all, Sam hadn't outwardly warmed to him and had pointedly asked him yesterday how long he was staying.

He wished he knew. He didn't want to stay. He wanted to move on before he got comfortable, but Justin kept catching up with him and telling him to stay just one more day, and he was already on day five just by not leaving. Anyway, he wasn't going to argue with Justin.

"If you have to," Sam muttered.

Not a great response, but what did he expect? Sam had every reason to be pissed at him.

"So I had this idea. It's probably nothing, but the family at table five, by the window, they haven't checked in yet and they've been driving all night. What if I go to the office and grab the keys and the welcome pack, then sit there with them as they eat lunch, and explain about the events and the programs and hand out maps in a conversation rather than a speech? I mean, they're exhausted." Sam leveled him with a glare, but Martin had no idea what it meant, and he felt as if he'd just fucked up completely, so he began to backtrack. "I know it's not what you probably do." What could he say that would possibly sell this to Sam? "Only I could talk them through the options for riding, up-sell, you know, and it would be a calm place here, where they could talk and..." He stopped and took a step back away from the counter because Sam was still staring. But he didn't seem angry or defensive or worried. Instead he looked confused.

"How did you know the meatballs have marjoram and rosemary or that the sauce was homemade?" Sam asked, finally.

Fuck, that was way off the subject. Was he being

accused of stealing a recipe or something? There was a book left behind the counter, a way for the staff to know what went into the food; common practice in any restaurant. Or at least that's what Martin had assumed when he'd cast a look over it at the start of his shift.

"I looked at the master list you have for staff. I'm sorry if that was the wrong thing to do."

"And you remember that kind of detail?"

Martin squirmed inside.

"I like meatballs," he offered. Any waiter worth his salt should recall ingredients, but maybe he'd overdone the explanation to the customer, given himself away, crossed some kind of non-chef kind of line.

"Okay. Also, your idea about checking them in as they sit in here is a good one. Go get their papers."

Martin felt warm at the tiny hint of approval from Sam.

The family was grateful, talking about the excellent customer service, and the little girl even demanded that it should be Martin who retied her laces. By the time he'd finished with the paperwork and issued the keys, their lunch was done, and Sam came right out and said that Martin should walk them to their cabin to explain where things were, and help them with their bags.

They attempted to tip him, but he declined as politely as he could and left them with the assurance that anyone would have done the same thing. What he'd done, helping them, left him with a smile he couldn't seem to shake.

When his shift ended, it was only three, and he actively sought out something else to do, which led to him being outside in the cool May air, knee deep in mud, assisting in fence repair. He recalled Nate mentioning that there was work in the stables if he ever got any spare time, and Martin jumped at the chance. Nate, the oldest Todd brother, and the go-to guy for the horses at Crooked Tree, was the strong silent type, and the master of inscrutable expressions. Martin loved that Nate was happy to work in peace. Together, they carried materials over the field to the fence at the rear, where the paddock stopped and the forest began. Just beyond, tucked into the trees, there was a new construction; a sprawling log cabin that seemed to be close to being finished. Martin wondered who it was for? *Some lucky person who is entitled to a home.*

They worked in silence for the most part, only covering the simple things like *'pass me the hammer'* or *'hold this steady'*, and not much else.

That was, until they were nearly done.

"You doin' okay?" Nate asked and leaned on the most recently finished part of the new fence, his boot on the first rail.

"Yep," Martin lied.

It seemed that was enough for Nate, as he went back to a silence that lasted until they were done. His muscles ached, but in a good way, through solid hard work. He and Nate had fallen into a rhythm, and when he stood back to check everything, he crossed his arms over his chest.

"See the depth we went there?" he asked.

"Yes."

"That's important. For next time." He side-eyed Martin and nodded.

Martin was quick to reassure him. "I'll remember."

Nate nodded, and picked up his jacket.

"Ten tomorrow, here, if Sam can spare you."

It wasn't as if he had assigned shifts anywhere on the ranch, but it did seem that Sam had been the one tasked with keeping him busy. Up until now at least. Maybe from today, he would be answering to Nate? Who the hell knew.

"Okay."

"You're done for today," Nate muttered and stalked away, and that was it. Martin had been dismissed.

Now what? He had space in a cabin with four rooms the ranch had for staff who needed accommodation. Only two were occupied—him and a chatty kid who was there for work experience and thought working on a ranch was the "coolest thing ever." Martin wanted to agree, but that would mean admitting he enjoyed slotting into this weird-ass support role.

And that was something he would never admit. Admitting that meant agreeing he had a place here and that the group of people he was with were worth working for. They were a family, Sam and Justin, Nate and Jay, the kids, Jay's sister, Nate's brothers, Adam, who wasn't there right now, Adam's partner who was Justin's brother, and the older generation. A real family.

Martin didn't hold much with family. Family was selfish and hurt you, left you, and fucked you over. Family was something someone like Martin read about in glossy magazines, and just because he hadn't seen arguments didn't mean they didn't exist.

He had a standing invite to grab food at Branches. All the staff did, entering through a back door and sitting at a table just off the kitchen. He never went. Instead, he'd taken to going into the small shop and grabbing sandwiches, which meant on day five of being at Crooked Tree he'd had ten sets of sandwiches. The only thing he took from the restaurant was coffee, and that was rare. They might not be paying him, but that didn't matter; he owed them all. Back in his room, sandwiches gone, sitting on his bed in the dark, staring out of a window that faced the trees, he felt wrong. He'd enjoyed working outside, but stuck in here, his skin too tight, he was hungry, tired, should have been happy and relaxed, and was instead tense and desperate to get outside. The same thing happened every damn night.

Back in Vermont, he'd had a room over the café, but that hadn't been where he'd slept all the time. On any night where it wasn't too cold, he was on the roof, where he'd strung a hammock and watched the stars until he fell asleep. Up there, he could forget how he'd ended up at the café, forget his fears and worries. Being outside had been the only reason he'd survived the fire that had consumed the entire building. If he'd been in his bed, he would never have made it out alive. He was lucky he hadn't broken something when he'd jumped from that building to the next. The thought of being trapped inside anywhere had always made him edgy, so he tried not to think about it, attempted to calm his breathing, focus on formulas or theorems—anything to get his brain back on track.

Tonight, not even solving math problems worked, and grabbing his coat, he left by the back door and kept to the shadows.

This side of the river he was away from the *family*, and if he was quick, he could leave the staff cabin, maybe cross the river higher up, and go for a walk to ease the tension in his chest.

It wasn't the warmest of nights, but bundled up in his coat, with enough layers, he might even be able to find somewhere to sit and stare at the stars. Fate wasn't interested in allowing him solitude though, and he had to stop himself from bolting when someone called from the darkness.

"Hey!"

He curtailed his desperate need to run and, instead, turned to face the owner of the voice, making out the features of the man he'd delivered groceries to. "Mr. Colby."

"Please, call me Tyler, and you're Martin, right? We met when you delivered my groceries, and of course you know that because you just called me Mr. Colby, which started this whole sentence."

"Uh-huh."

Tyler moved closer, and under the bright moon, Martin could make out his smile and the shape of him in shadows. He had a bag in his hand, a large bag that appeared to be weighing him down.

"I bet you think I'm moving a body," Tyler joked, dropping the bag, where it thudded as it met the ground. Martin hadn't for one minute considered that Tyler had a body in the bag, but now he'd said it, that was all Martin could imagine. "I'm not. It's stones, is all. Rocks... I'm a geologist, well, kind of. That isn't my official title. I actually work in seismology, and I wanted to take some rocks back to my cabin because then I can get a feel for the kind of land we're sitting on."

He finished his explanation with an expansive wave of his hands. Was he expecting an answer? In a social situation like this, Martin should show interest, right? He should ask questions, but his mind was blank. This was what happened when he was faced with a hot man. He became tongue-tied, and panicky, and ended up fucking things up.

And there was no denying that Tyler was way up there on the scale of sexy-hot. Actually, right near the top of the chart. He not only looked good, but when they'd got close in the kitchen, he'd smelled good, and his smile was stunning. Martin was attracted to him, and confused by him, and wished he could just vanish in a hole in the ground.

Tyler kept talking, utterly unaware of Martin's growing panic. "I think I have some granodiorite in here. It's a plutonic igneous rock intermediate in composition between granite and diorite, not that you need to know that, but it's interesting." Tyler paused again.

"Okay," Martin murmured.

Tyler forged ahead as if that was permission for him to keep talking. He wore glasses and kept pushing them up his nose. He was a contradiction, half genius, half sexy man with his earnest unapologetic focus only making him hotter.

"I picked up too many. They're damn heavy. I couldn't leave it though because what if I go back the wrong way and I forget where I'd seen it? So this is me, standing in the dark with what looks like a bag with a dead body, rambling nonsense." He bent to pick up the bag, made it a couple of feet, and dropped it again.

"Can I help?" Martin asked, waiting for the smile of approval, the acknowledgment from Tyler that he was being helpful, and felt a warmth trickle inside him when Tyler grinned.

"Please." He unzipped the bag and lifted out what looked like a large common rock and then strained to pass it to Martin. "If you could take the granodiorite, that would be helpful."

Martin took the heavy weight and held it close to his chest, his jacket getting stuck up and under it. Tyler spent a while helping him pull it down, his touch firm, his focus intense. The scent of the man was intoxicating, and Martin groaned inwardly. Allowing himself to be attracted to the hot cute nerd wasn't a good idea.

They headed to the river bank and followed the path back to Tyler's cabin. Tyler didn't talk much, which was a good thing as far as Martin was concerned because he felt off-balance and a little afraid. Not of Tyler, but of the spark of attraction that had ignited inside him when Tyler had had his head bent close and was fixing Martin's coat. He'd been so close that Martin could have reached out and touched him. Although then he would have dropped the rock, probably on his foot, knowing his luck.

When they reached Tyler's door, Martin placed the rock on the porch and backed away, ready to leave immediately.

"Wait, would you like a beer?" Tyler asked. "I have beer, which you know because you packed it away, but maybe you thought I'd drunk it all, so you wouldn't have expected… shit, I'm rambling again. Come in, I'll get us a beer and give you a proper thank you."

Martin didn't follow Tyler inside, even if his thoughts did turn X-rated at the offer of a proper thank you.

What is wrong with me? I'm not here to lust after the guests. He was confused at the attraction, and he hovered at the door waiting for Tyler to come back so he could explain that he didn't want to go in. Hell, it was hard enough handling time with the owners of this place, let alone more random strangers. Never mind how nice their voices were or the fact that Tyler Colby was... yeah...

When Tyler returned, he pulled the door shut behind him, still in his bulky coat, and with two beers in hand. Clearly they weren't going inside at all, and all of Martin's worries about what he would say had been for nothing. Tyler held out one of the bottles to Martin.

"I don't drink," Martin said, firmly.

Tyler didn't push. If anything, he seemed relieved and placed both bottles, unopened, on the ground by the door. "It's nice to have company," he said and sat on one of the big Adirondack chairs. Martin leaned back on the porch surround, just to have something to hold on to. "Sit down. Tell me what it's like being a cowboy on a ranch?"

All Martin could think was what would a normal person do in these circumstances? *Well, to start, idiot, they would have taken the beer and not made a huge thing about not drinking.* Then after that, nursing the full bottle, he could sit down and talk about everything and nothing.

"I'm sorry. I need to go," Martin excused himself and left before Tyler could say anything else.

There was no point asking what a normal person would do because he clearly wasn't normal at all.

Chapter Five

AT THE BREAKFAST PLANNING MEETING, WITH NATE, JAY, and Gabe around the table, Tyler watched the discussion unfold. Nate was angry and Jay had taken the role of placating his upset partner.

"I'm not having drones on the ranch again," Nate repeated for what must have been the third time, and Tyler winced at Nate's horrified expression. It wasn't as if he'd suggested that they close down the ranch to continue surveys. Everything had been going well until he'd casually mentioned that he'd be happy to give the ranch copies of any drone footage he took so they could use it in marketing. He was halfway through explaining how cool it was to see places from up high when Nate had gone into semi-shock, pushed his chair back, and jumped up.

"No more drones," he'd snapped. "Your people messed with my horses, and I won't have that again."

The *people* that Nate mentioned would have spent the longest time collecting data and might well have run roughshod over the ranch, but he couldn't speak for them. "We have the original ground surveys, but with shifts in the terrain, we need to undertake a limited aerial survey of the site itself," Tyler explained. "I need to get up and take some—"

"More drones wasn't part of the deal," Nate interrupted and began to pace the small office. "Your office said you'd be off-site and we wouldn't even know you were here. But if you're using drones, you'll scare the horses, and what about our guests? They'll accuse us of invading their privacy. Jay, sort this out."

Jay glanced at him and then to Tyler. "Nate's right; I'm not sure we signed up for more drone usage."

"Fuck, was it in the contract we signed?" Nate looked at Jay, who frowned at him.

"No, it wasn't," Jay said.

Tyler held up his hands. "This would be remote to the ranch, nowhere near the horses or guests, and actually there wasn't a real contract signed as such for us to be on the land. You know we can go to a site if it's in public interest."

Jay narrowed his eyes, but he couldn't argue that point. The Bureau had decided that the far western side of Crooked Tree was a prime location for the station, and had sought enough agreement to make sure the landowner knew what to expect. They didn't need a formal agreement at this level, and the disruption would be small anyway. That didn't mean Tyler was going to ride roughshod over Nate or the others, despite them having little choice in his being there.

"Have a cake." Gabe interrupted Nate's pacing and thrust the plate of cakes under his nose. Gabe was Nate's brother and the less emotional of the two, it seemed. Mention horses and that was Nate's territory, and one he guarded jealously.

Gabe continued to talk. "He didn't mean he'd use the drones where it would affect us." Nate threw a quick look at Tyler, who nodded immediately. Nate took a slice of lemon drizzle cake and sat again; he didn't actually eat the cake, but it had been a good tactic from his brother to get him to calm down. Once he was sure everyone was settled, Tyler carried on.

"The footage would exclusively be of the area where we plan to install."

Nate muttered something, but he was too far away for Tyler to hear him.

"And the supplies you need hauling up there?" Gabe changed the subject, and Tyler was grateful for that, given the way Nate was glaring at him.

"The office said they spoke to you about hiring in someone for the week to help with transport and support? Or maybe you can spare a staff member? They said I should talk to you."

"We have it covered," Jay said.

"We do?" Nate sounded surprised.

Nate sent him a look that spoke volumes, but Tyler was too focused to wonder what that all meant.

Tyler spread out another map and cleared his throat. "Okay, that's good. Right now, I'd like some advice on getting to the exact place I need to be," he said and gently nudged the map toward Nate. "I imagine we'll take this off road to as close as we can. What do you think?"

Nate peered at the map, cake crumbs falling onto it, which he brushed away. "West Seven. That's part of the Springs complex, so as I said to your office, you'll have difficulty with full vehicular access, but depending where you place the *thing*, then we should be able to get close."

The seismic station with seismometer, digitizer, and electronics buried in a polypropylene vault, plus a surface-level solar panel and satellite dish was more than just a *thing*. It was two hundred thousand dollars' worth of equipment, and Tyler had jumped through official hoops to get agreement for the installation. He wasn't going to remind Nate of that though and waited for more.

Nate trailed his finger along a line on the map, then tapped at something thoughtfully. "Used to be an old cabin there; at least I recall one from when I was a kid. Also ground water; you'll want to watch that."

"I know the terrain," Tyler said. "The stability of the land at this point is what led me to Crooked Tree, but I'm aware of the issues with the water table."

Nate nodded, evidently respecting what Tyler was saying. "Let's talk logistics then. You have the off-road vehicle. I can give you detailed information about the place you need, but then you're on your own."

"Apart from Martin," Jay said, and the room went silent as Nate choked on his bite of cake. Gabe patted him on the back, but he was looking at Jay, and his expression was that of a very confused man.

"What do you mean, Martin?" he finally said and thumped Nate again.

Martin? Wasn't that the guy who'd helped him with the rock, the one who'd run off after the offer of a beer? Unless there were two Martins working on the ranch, which was statistically possible. The thought of the Martin he knew being his company for the next week was one that filled him with equal parts trepidation and anticipation. How many times last night had he wanted to bury his hands in Martin's soft curls and hold on tight while kissing him like there was no tomorrow?

And, as to helping Martin *off* with his coat as opposed to unsnagging it from the rock? Yep, that was on Tyler's to-do list after last night. There was so much emotion in Martin's expression: curiosity and fear and possibly even a spark of attraction? That was wishful thinking, but if it had been there, then maybe some hot sex in a tent could be in the cards? Tyler couldn't recall the last time he'd... oh yeah, he did. Yan Evers, fellow research scientist, June, a pretty satisfying one-night stand after the Earth Interior seminar in Massachusetts. That was, God, nearly a whole damn year ago. Since then, it had been his active imagination, coupled with his right hand. Actual sex? Actual kissing? With an actual man as appealing as the quiet Martin? Now *that* was worth thinking about.

It was Jay's turn to clear his throat, which snapped him out of his woolgathering. There was tension in the room, Nate facing off against Jay, muttering something about how in hell Martin was on the list of possibles, and that he'd do it if he could take his horse.

Jay finally pressed a hand to Nate's chest. "Listen to me, Nate. It was Justin who suggested that Martin be the one who accompanies Tyler to site and camps there to assist because Ethan and Adam are coming home earlier than expected, and Justin needs time."

A hundred things passed silently between Jay, Nate, and Gabe, each man apparently working through something that was way over Tyler's head. Finally it was Gabe who spoke.

"Okay then," he said. "That's decided, Martin will go with you."

IT TURNED out that Martin definitely *was* the same guy who had dropped off his groceries and helped him carry a rock, and abruptly the idea of spending time alone in the wilds of Montana sounded much more fun. Okay, so Martin didn't talk a lot, and he was closed off and private, but Tyler decided his own personal brand of charm would be enough to finally break through the man's shell. It didn't have to lead to sex or to hand jobs or even kissing; it could just be friendship. Martin was so easy on the eyes, and as he helped to load the Jeep, his muscles bunched and released in all kinds of interesting ways. Not that Tyler would make it obvious he was looking. It was just the odd cautious glance that was part of his way of sizing a person up.

Martin didn't smile, but he worked harder and longer than any other man standing at the loading zone who were joking about the wilderness and survival rates. Even Nate was joining in, although Tyler wondered if that was him making sure 'Tyler and his damn drone' left without causing problems. When they were all done with the technical equipment, it was just food that needed to be loaded. The location was a good five-hour drive from there, and there was no point in them coming back and forth for provisions, so they had containers of meals, cereals, cans, emergency rations, and while they stayed fresh, a supply of cookies, cake, and biscuits.

The generator fit snugly next to the small camping stove and a backup supply of gas, and there were the parts for a bathroom tent, complete with a makeshift shower and a portable composting toilet. Tyler loved his work, he loved camping, but gone were the days when he would curl on the ground next to a fire and dream of the earth beneath him. He wanted a cot, a toilet, and somewhere to get clean, and that was non-negotiable. He expected to get rough around the edges, but hell, he wanted *some* comfort when he spent quiet evenings staring at the stars.

Which had him wondering if Martin was the kind of man who liked to stare at the big open sky. Was he someone who would want to talk about the stars? Or the sky? Or geology? Or was he a sports kind of guy, in which case the conversation would be one-sided as Tyler wasn't a follower of any teams worth noting.

Finally it was time to do the last-minute checking of lists and the itinerary, and then there was nothing holding them there. Martin deferred to him to drive, but that was okay; he'd driven worse terrain than this backcountry. The easy bit was getting off the ranch complex, and they took narrow tracks past cabins, staying at a low speed in deference to the guests. Then it became harder as they headed out and up over meadows that changed to become a climb, with rocky outcrops. The satellite mapping system gave them a clear direction, but it took a lot of concentration to get this far.

"You doing okay?" Tyler asked after the first half hour of complete silence.

Martin glanced at him and nodded. The action loosened curls that he'd tucked behind his ear, and he pushed them back. His eyes were an intriguing shade of icy green, pale and rimmed with the darkest and longest lashes that Tyler had ever seen on a man. Add the softness of his lips and the darkening stubble, and the package that was Martin, kind of skinny but sexy, was gorgeous.

"If you want to drive…" Tyler suggested, but now Martin shook his head and turned face front, the huge paper map backing up the satellite navigation system gripped hard on his lap. The rocks smoothed out as they drove over the plane, and for want of anything else to do, he began to talk.

"Right here, there used to be a huge lake, did you know that?"

Tyler saw Martin peer out of the side window, so at least he was showing interest, but still he didn't talk. It was going to be a long week if he was working alongside someone who didn't enter into discussions, so he carried on.

"There was a glacier in the last ice age, and it blocked this valley, just like the one down at Lake Missoula. Have you ever been to Lake Missoula?"

Martin shook his head.

Tyler sighed at the memories of his time at the Lake. "I spent an entire summer there, with an ex. He was another geologist though, and even though we were an item, we disagreed on the water depths that were exposed by the laminated rocks." He realized what he'd explained, and Martin shot him a look, but it wasn't one of disgust or disdain. If anything, he appeared mildly curious.

Tyler would take that over indifference or condemnation any day.

"Anyway, we didn't last long after the summer. He was an arrogant ass. You know the type." He cleared his throat, aware he needed to stop talking. Then he stopped the car and pointed up at the sloping sides of the valley. "So, at Lake Missoula, a lobe of ice crept south and blocked the Clark Fork River. That's right near present-day Sandpoint, Idaho. A huge lake of glacial water formed behind the obstruction, and you can see the steps in the hillside. Just like here. Can you see them?" When Martin didn't seem to be checking it out, Tyler prompted him again.

"You need to look at them to understand what I mean."

Martin shot him a pointed look then, turning back to stare at the steps in the land. "I'm looking," he said.

"Okay, so they're actually the old shorelines of the lake, at all its different levels, steps eroded away by the ebbs and flows of water. Missoula was over four thousand feet deep. I don't think this one was as deep as that. Still, it's pretty cool, right, to see the steps and know that where we are was under thousands of feet of water. What do you think?"

There, he'd asked the silent man a question, and in a normal situation, the other person would give an answer.

"Cool," Martin murmured, still staring out of the side of the Jeep.

"Tough audience," Tyler said with a smile. "Now, what else can I tell you that's interesting. Oh yeah, you see how we were driving over undulations in the ground, like up and down? When the glacier melted just that bit too much, the same as at Missoula, the entire lake here abruptly emptied, and these layers were ripples caused by the departing water. The prairie ranch road we're on goes over the evidence there was even a lake here to start with. If you get a drone, you can look down and actually see the rise in the terrain and then the fall, like a giant has dropped a stone into a pond."

"A giant," Martin murmured after a short pause.

"Yep, a giant. A big fuck-off giant dropped all these boulders as well." Tyler pointed at the boulder next to the car. "A giant glacier deposited those, carried them for miles, and then dropped them as the ice split. They're all over the prairies, and we call them Drop Stones."

Martin shot him a look that spoke volumes, as if Tyler was boring, but Tyler wasn't an educator without reason. He loved geology, got excited about every single layer of mud and stone beneath his feet, and if Martin was going to sit there silent, then Tyler was going to damn well fill the silence with the sound of his own voice.

"We use varves and rhythmites to unravel a lake's past; deposits are laminated. That means layered like in pastry. The river silts are lighter in color, and glacial lake sediments are darker. Fascinating, right? Also, there is rock flour all around here, where stones were crumbled from erosion, and some of the smaller rocks, if you apply enough pressure, will disintegrate in your hand. Rock flour isn't exactly like flour, not fine deposits. Sometimes it can be entire strata in a cliff face." He clicked his fingers. "Oh, and I know you said you haven't been to Lake Missoula, but when the lake drained violently, the currents scoured out the depression that holds Dog Lake. Awesome walks around Dog Lake. Do you like walking?"

"Yes," Martin murmured. "Shouldn't we get going so we reach the campsite while we still have light?"

That was possibly the longest sentence that Martin had uttered since getting in the car, and for a brief moment, it threw Tyler.

"You're right." Tyler edged forward, and they continued on their way.

I won't let one taciturn cowboy mess with my head. I'm going to enjoy the hell out of this. Martin could either join in or not. It didn't make any odds, because Tyler had done plenty of isolated fieldwork since he'd been big enough to understand his world; probably around the age of three. He had his mom and dad to thank for that, and he would be forever grateful.

Chapter Six

Martin was thrown; Tyler specifically said he had an ex-boyfriend. Not that it mattered. After all, there wasn't any reason that he would find Martin attractive. Not to mention that Martin wasn't ever letting his guard down with a man again.

Not after Levi.

Levi with his bright blue eyes and long dark hair and the softest kisses. Levi, who had stolen his heart and wound up dead. The only person Martin had ever truly loved.

Levi had been a long time ago now, and Martin forced aside the insistent push of memories and instead focused on Tyler.

The main thing Martin knew about him was that Tyler didn't stop talking. It seemed as if he was intent on filling the silence, and that implied he thought Martin's stillness was a bad thing. Martin craved silence and hadn't come to terms with the fact that he was even on this *expedition* with the smiling, loud, confident Tyler Colby.

Not that he'd had a choice about going.

Or at least the choice had been pretty loose. It was either work with Nate and the horses or spend a week in a tent on a remote part of the ranch with a total stranger. Given the way Nate was still in the wary-of-him stage, he was happy to be volunteered. He was here to be a packhorse, lift, carry, arrange, put up tents, help with the digging, and apparently there was a wage at the end of it, funded by the Earthquake Study Center, or whatever it was called. Maybe it would be enough to put away so he could move on from Crooked Tree. After all he only needed bus fare and maybe enough cash to get a couple of rooms on the way to the ocean.

Sam had been another person to avoid. He'd gone from hostile and worried to being overly interested in Martin's life; the parts that Martin didn't want to talk about: the pain, the hardship, the abuse, the murders. He couldn't understand why Sam wanted to know what it had been like for Martin growing up; it wasn't as if Sam needed that information for any practical reason. Unless understanding young-Martin would allow Sam to come to terms with what teenage-Martin had become and how it had affected Justin. Maybe it was a messed-up need to understand Martin, but there was honestly nothing left inside him that could ever make things right.

He was so lost in thought, lulled by the rhythm of the tires on the grass, and so tangled up in the mess in his head that he hadn't even realized the vehicle had stopped.

"I just need to get my bearings," Tyler explained and left the car with what looked like an iPad. He stood outside, turning three-sixty and then nodding. "It's okay.

We're heading in the right direction. Now, come look at this."

Martin didn't want to get out of the car. Whatever Tyler was going to show him wasn't going to be as cool as Tyler expected it to be. Unless it was to explain the navigation system and the mapping that would reveal their final destination. Because at the end of this drive was the lure of regular hard work and then sleeping in his own tent or maybe right out under the stars. May brought slightly warmer weather. At least the ground snow had gone for now, but sleeping outside was not going to be likely. *A man can hope.*

"Come on," Tyler called, and finally Martin couldn't avoid it any longer. He clambered down from the high seat and walked to the back of the vehicle, where Tyler was messing about inside one of his cases. "This is the drone we use I want to show you…" He picked it up carefully, did what seemed like preflight checks, and then, using a control on the iPad, he shot the small gray drone directly into the air. He tutted and murmured and pushed back the errant hair that fell on his forehead before finally beaming widely.

Jesus, that smile was incendiary.

"Look," he demanded and held the iPad a little away from himself. Martin reached for it, but Tyler shook his head. "You need to come closer. I can't let this go."

The drone whined away above them, and Martin finally leaned in. Tyler traced the pattern with a finger. The screen showed what the drone's camera was seeing, and he could see the top of the Jeep, but not them; they were too small. What he could see were what looked like ripples, and actually they were exactly as Tyler told him they would be.

"Where the giant dropped his stone," Tyler said and moved the drone behind them until it hovered in a particular spot, and right there was the epicenter of the ripples.

Martin wanted to make a comment, but this close-proximity thing was messing with his head. Up close, he could feel the warmth of Tyler, smell the citrusy freshness of his scent, and see the start of stubble darkening his jawline. Up this close, it was too much, and he stepped back and away when it became more than he could handle.

Tyler shot him a puzzled glance, and at this point, Martin knew he should say something. *Anything.*

"That's interesting," he offered and then headed back to the Jeep.

When Tyler climbed back in, he sighed. "Sorry, I know I get carried away."

Make him feel better, tell Tyler it's all okay, and that you moved away because you are completely fucked up, and that you have no idea to handle social interactions like this.

Instead, Martin shrugged because yet again, words failed him. He was coming across as a rude asshole who couldn't be bothered with anything real, and he hated himself so badly for being that person. What was he going to say? What was the point in starting a conversation with someone when he knew nothing about the subject?

Best off keeping ya' mouth shut, boy.

His dad's words were never far away; they formed the soundtrack to his entire damned life.

They completed the rest of the journey without

talking, although Tyler selected music and sang along to it. Clearly he needed noise as much as Martin didn't.

When they neared the site, the terrain became more treacherous, less undulating prairie and more boulders and cliff edges. The Jeep made good work of crunching over most things, and Tyler was more than competent when it came to driving; another thing to envy about the put-together man.

The going was slow, and Tyler turned down the music, concentrating on the track and every so often checking the satellite system, looking for their geo-tag and ensuring they were heading in the right direction.

Martin just held on for the ride.

Finally, the dot that was them loosely managed to match up to the location they needed, and that was as far as they could get with the Jeep. The remainder was maybe four hundred yards up the hill, over the creek, and into the hollow of the mountain. That was why Martin was here. He was the one tasked with trekking everything up there. But not tonight. They were an hour from darkness, and pitching the tents down here and setting a base camp was priority number one.

At least he knew how to set up a tent.

Not only was it a mathematical issue to get corners right, but he'd grown up learning how to survive in the wilderness, and that included the skill of putting up a tent.

His dad lived by the conviction that one day the US would descend into an anarchy that he himself had created. It would be *him* who destroyed the government, undermined society, and restarted the United States as something very different. He'd expected there to be a loss of electrical supply, of vital supplies—in fact he'd counted on it—and had known hunting and survival skills were vital.

Then one day he'd had thrown his five-year-old son, Jamie, out of the cabin with a pup tent and nothing else.

You'll live or die, I ain't got no time for sickly useless kids.

Martin remembered each syllable that his dad spat at him; they revisited him in his nightmares.

Martin had survived that night in the tangled wilds of Colorado, and his dad had been so proud of him, said he was a champ, praised him to the others who were part of Martin's extended family. There was no sign of his mom or baby sister when he got home, but he'd never questioned that, and soon it became the norm that it was just him, Dad, and the other survivalists. Some of the other men had girlfriends; none of them lasted long, but some of them tried to be a mom to Martin for as long as they'd stayed.

He'd soon realized he didn't need a mom and that he wanted to be left alone. Only in therapy did he come to terms with that the night Martin survived outside was the same night he'd misplaced part of his humanity and lost the only family that might have saved him.

"Where do we start?" Tyler prompted, and Martin shook himself back to the here and now.

"I got this," he said and began to unload the Jeep of the camping items, the tents, bedrolls, camping stove, the gas until he had a methodical pile of things in the center of a clear area.

"I can do my own tent." Tyler began to lay out what he needed, and in silence, they erected each tent, maybe six feet apart, sideways on the hill in a hollow so they were protected and also on level ground. A third tent would be used to house the scientific work that Tyler was undertaking, and a fourth for the bathroom.

Martin collected small rocks, piling them into a circle, realizing he was testing each one for strength after the explanation of what rock flour was. Then he made a fire and set up the small generator, ready to cook some of their supplies. Something else he was good at was foraging, but the only scavenging he'd be doing here was to rummage through the dinners that Sam had sent them off with.

Tonight was stew, beef, one packet, and biscuits that would only stay fresh for today and possibly tomorrow.

"Wow, look at that view," Tyler stood, hands on hips, staring out from the camp. Sunset was nearing its end, the pinks and oranges fading into the gray smudge of night, and Tyler was right. It *was* beautiful. Tyler zipped up his coat and joined Martin, opening the small chair in the place that would be their home by the fire for the next week.

They ate in silence, but Martin knew it wouldn't last long.

"So, how long have you been a cowboy?" Tyler asked, scooping out the last of the stew in his bowl.

"I'm not a cowboy. I just shift things around."

"Oh, okay," Tyler said and then looked around him. "Do you enjoy your work?"

"It's work," Martin replied. Then before Tyler could ask him any more damn questions, he held out a hand for Tyler's plate and headed toward the noise of water. He'd seen the stream when they'd arrived; it ran maybe twenty feet from the tents and widened around boulders before narrowing and then vanishing underground lower down the hill. Plates in one hand, flashlight in the other, he picked his way over the uneven ground, and finally, blessedly, he reached the water and a rock he could sit on.

Cold out here in the more exposed ground, he buried his face in his scarf and listened to the bubbling of water. More than once today he'd wanted to continue a conversation with Tyler, maybe ask a question, but what was the point? He'd likely ask the wrong thing or make a fool of himself. He had a degree, one he'd earned with blood, sweat and tears from night classes, but he wasn't a doctor of a subject like Doctor Tyler Colby, and who the hell would want to hear about Martin's love of math? Math might well inspire Martin, but it was a dry subject, not sexy like geology and earthquakes and freaking ripples left by glaciers.

Tyler was a nice guy. Interesting. Sexy and easy on the eyes and all the things that Martin thought he should have been attracted to if he was *normal.*

Which he wasn't. The last time he'd been normal, he was five. The only time he'd acted on his impulses, he'd been thirteen, and that was never happening again.

Maybe what he needed to do was go back to the tents and explain that he didn't want to talk about geology, only because he was tired and had too much crap in his head right now to remember how to be normal. So much for finding peace and keeping all his demons at bay. This enforced proximity with Tyler was dangerous.

Okay, one more minute, and then I'll go back and try to interact without coming off as a fucking idiot.

"What if he asks me questions? If I talk to him, he'll ask me things I can't answer. Things I don't want to answer."

His whisper vanished into the cold, swallowed by the noise of the water, and he slumped where he sat, his dad's voice a devious creeping pain in his head.

No one wants to hear your crap, boy, none of your fucking nonsense. Get my belt.

"Fuck my life."

Chapter Seven

Tyler went to find Martin after five minutes. He gave him that long to reasonably find the water and wash the plates, but anything more than that, and he began to imagine Martin had fallen into the water or broken his leg or something worse. Being good at imagining the worst kept him safe, but he'd only had himself to look after before. Now he had another person working with him in a remote space, where anything could happen.

Martin intrigued him. All those soft curls tumbling to brush his shoulders, and bangs long enough to hide his eyes if needed. Which was often. There was something about the man that Tyler needed to know more about. Maybe it was the silence or the odd glances he would give Tyler that spoke of vulnerability and shyness. Then there had been the tension in him when they'd stood close checking images from the drone. Martin clearly hadn't wanted to stand there, but was it because Tyler was doing his thing of boring someone to death, or was it something else?

He didn't have to look too hard to see the wariness in Martin; it was right on the surface in every micro-expression, in every casual step away from Tyler to give them distance, and that fascinated him as if Martin was a puzzle waiting to be solved.

Martin wasn't a cowboy. He shifted things. That was how he'd explained himself, but there was more to him, intelligence in his eyes as he looked at the images, and Tyler wondered if questions were on the tip of his tongue.

Wishful thinking that the sexy guy with the curls and the gorgeous green eyes would actually be interested in geology.

"Fuck my life," the words drifted his way, the curse loud, the pain in each word obvious. Martin was perched on a large drop stone, his feet dangling above the fast-flowing water in the shallow creek. The light of Tyler's flashlight illuminated the path, and he was relieved that Martin didn't seem injured.

"Hey," Tyler said when he grew closer.

"Hey," Martin answered but didn't move from his perch.

"You're sitting on a drop stone, like the ones I talked about before." He was trying for light conversation.

"Right," Martin said.

"May I join you?" Tyler didn't wait for an answer at first, but as he went to sit next to Martin, he hesitated. If only he could get a handle on him, then he might know a way to break all these silences. "Is that okay?" he asked again.

"I was just leaving," Martin said and hopped down off the rock, collecting the plates and heading back to the camp. Tyler went after him, jogging a little to catch up, his flashlight bobbling a line of light that kept his steps on even ground.

"Wait up, Martin," he called, and after a moment's pause Martin stopped walking and turned to face him. Tyler dropped the beam of his flashlight so it was directed at Martin's feet rather than his face.

"Yes?" he asked, but it wasn't angry; it was an exasperated sound.

"I talk too much. I like company. We need a safe word."

"A what now?" Martin said and took a step away, stumbling a little and righting himself.

"No, not in a sex way, I didn't mean like that." He let out an exasperated huff. "I didn't explain it well. What I mean is, if I'm talking too much, just say the safe word, and I'll back off. Say bananas or something. Don't worry. I'll listen and stop. My mom always said I could talk the hind legs off a—"

"Banana," Martin muttered.

"Oh, is that you practicing, or you mean I should stop—"

"Banana."

They stood in the dark, and Tyler had no idea what to say next when abruptly, Martin snorted a laugh. "Bed," he said and turned back in the direction of the tents. Tyler was too wired to get into his tent, and certainly there would be no sleep just yet. He'd remembered to pack his Kindle, but he was more interested in the most recent seismic readings from Yellowstone. There was always seismic activity in Montana, which had been the premise for the investigations that had brought him here to this point on

Crooked Tree. It had interested him to see a seismic belt form far from an active plate tectonic boundary, and that was based on a global assessment. The original systems built to track seismic activity hadn't considered a monitoring station this far out until Tyler had followed his instincts and provided proof of what was needed right here to deal with the unpredictability of earthquakes.

He moved his iPad to the entrance to his tent and sat on the seat to flick to the most recent bare-earth Lidar images of his location. The land surface was portrayed in detail, and he traced the line of the active seismic fault with the potential to trigger a magnitude 6.5 to 7.5 earthquake. Every expert had imagined this area was relatively immune to large earthquakes; everyone knew the fault existed, but the best available evidence was that it was not active, and no earthquakes had been traced to this point. Until Tyler's research.

He'd begged, cajoled, blackmailed, and finally persuaded the right people that a new monitoring station be added to the network covering Western Montana, and a long and frustrating year later he was here to do the work.

Excitement spurred him on to look at more data, and only when he yawned and realized it was nearly ten, that the fire had died out, and the cold had frozen inside him, did he move away from the flap. Then he went back out to check the fire was truly out and that everything was secure in the Jeep, and finally he crawled into his sleeping bag off the ground on the small cot. He wore so many layers that it was difficult to roll over, so he stayed where he was, staring at the roof of his tent, and as he drifted to sleep, thoughts of work and earthquakes and rocks slipped away until only his attraction to the enigmatic Martin remained in his mind.

Chapter Eight

DAWN LIGHTENED THE TENT ENOUGH TO PULL MARTIN from sleep, and he rolled to his side and stretched. They had a lot to do today: moving the technical equipment from the Jeep, transferring it to the approved site, and beginning to construct what was needed. He'd only looked at the parts briefly, aware he didn't actually have to know what he was doing. After all, he was only providing the muscle.

He also needed to get the fourth tent finished. He'd put it up last night and installed the toilet, but the shower part was more complicated. Luxuries like that hadn't been available to him as a kid, and he'd actually never seen a setup for camping like this. He had instructions though, and in the gentle early morning light, he pulled what he needed from the Jeep and began to construct the shower inside the bathroom tent. There was a tiny heater, pipes, and a large basin to stand in, and when he had it put together, he carried the water containers to the stream and filled them as best he could.

Once back, he tested the system out with cold water, satisfied that this worked and then he headed out of the tent, and the scent of bacon hit him head-on. Tyler was up, in jeans and a bulky sweater, standing by a new fire, poking at the wood.

"Morning," Martin said as he drew closer and was amused when Tyler shot up in the air in surprise.

"Jesus, you need a bell," he said and grabbed his chest in an exaggerated move. "And good morning. We have bacon. Every morning should start with bacon, don't you think?"

"And coffee," Martin added. "Mostly coffee."

Tyler held out a mug. "Already on it."

The coffee was dark, fragrant, and exactly what Martin needed to kick-start his day, and when he sat on his small chair opposite Tyler with a plate of bacon and biscuits, he couldn't have been happier. Not to mention the view from there was perfect. Not of the mountains beyond or the rolling grass or even the water shimmering in the daylight, though. No, the view was all about stealing glances at a rumpled and grinning Tyler. He was a sight for sore eyes, his hair fluffy from sleep, his hazel eyes sparkling with excitement, and he was smiling even as he ate his bacon. He had so much unbridled enthusiasm in him for what he was doing; so much excitement. It was a good look on a man.

"Have you been up long?" Tyler asked.

Martin had to remember how to talk when he'd slipped into pretending-not-to-stare mode for so long. "A while. The bathroom tent is finished and the shower works. I didn't check if the heater worked, but I don't imagine it was meant to sustain long luxurious hours under steaming hot water."

"Shame." Tyler laughed. "I love standing under a hot shower for hours if I have something to keep me busy." He winked then, but it wasn't flirting or a come-on. It was just buddies joking. Right? Not that they were buddies, or that Martin thought he knew how to handle anything like being a buddy.

Martin focused back on the bacon and again took point in cleaning the empty plates, leaving them to dry outside the tent. They each used the bathroom, but it took a long time for Martin to truly relax. It was a tent on the side of a mountain; it felt... wrong. At least he could wash up and face the world with something like a fresh face and bright attitude. There was no way he was letting any blackness creep up on him while he was out here. He wouldn't be any good to anyone if he was rocking in a corner whimpering about his shit life.

Then it was the two of them working to empty the Jeep. After the fifth journey up the hill carrying heavy boxes, the four hundred yards felt like miles. Tyler had stayed up there, cataloguing and working with equipment to locate the spot where the installation would be. Some of the items that he took up were awkwardly shaped, others in tiny boxes; quite a few were stamped *fragile*. On the other hand, the shovels and gravel were something that he could get behind using.

"That's the last of it," he advised as soon as the Jeep was empty. "What next?"

"Hmm?" Tyler looked up from his crouched position and blinked back to reality. Wherever he'd been was probably bursting full of technical information, and now he had to switch to telling Martin what to do next.

"Sorry to interrupt your thinking. Everything is up here now, so what's next?"

Tyler stood and brushed at the seat of his jeans. "Next is coffee and a muffin if there are any in the supplies. I can't work on an empty stomach, and bacon was a long time ago. Come on, I'll make us some, and I can explain what we need to complete today."

Martin followed Tyler, his calf muscles sore from all the trekking up and down the incline. He'd grown soft; it used to be he could trek for days without stopping, but working in a coffee shop had taken a toll on his love of walking for mile upon mile. Tyler made coffee and sat on his chair.

"So let me explain a bit about what we're doing."

Martin settled in for another essay, the word banana on the tip of his tongue only until Tyler started talking about earthquakes and the detail was interesting to hear.

"Montana has a history of earthquakes, but it's not as publicized as, say, earthquakes in LA or volcanoes in Yellowstone. Ask anyone who's been to the movies to see a disaster movie, and an earthquake in the ass end of Montana will never make the list of what they covered. Apart from a BBC movie about the Yellowstone super volcano. But the only thing that movie got right was the volcano was capable of burying states like Wyoming with volcanic ash and set off all kinds of seismic reactions beneath our feet. So yeah, earthquake action all over the state. Scary, right?"

"Yeah." What else could Martin say. He loved a good disaster movie but hadn't caught one about a super volcano.

"Sorry, I'm getting off topic." Tyler took a breath. "Actually, some earthquakes here are so large they can cause extensive damage, and they're happening all the time." He placed his hands next to each other. "An earthquake happens when rock underground abruptly breaks along a fault. When two blocks of rock are rubbing against each other, they stick," He moved his hands quickly and then stopped them at an angle to each other, probably to indicate the movement of the rocks he was describing. It didn't matter what he did with his hands, because Martin was fixated by the passion in his expression and wanted to focus on his face. "When the rocks break, that is when an earthquake happens. So all this sudden release of energy causes seismic waves. I mean, that is what makes the ground shake."

It sounded to Martin as if Tyler was using words with limited syllables, probably imagining that Martin wouldn't understand anything too technical. There was no way he was going to disabuse that notion, because then he'd have to explain how he'd gotten his degree in math, and elaborate on how his freaky brain worked.

"Okay," Martin offered when he realized Tyler was waiting for some kind of acknowledgment of what he'd said so far. "Two rocks, rub, catch, break, earthquake."

Tyler beamed at him, and a warmth sparked inside Martin's chest. Stupid how he so desperately needed approval from this man.

Tyler spoke with authority and great enthusiasm. "Some of the faults are actually visible, like the San Andreas Fault, which is a continental transform fault—it forms the tectonic boundary between plates." He did the movement thing with his hand again and finished it off with opening and closing his hands as if he was miming explosions. "But other earthquakes occur along faults that don't reach the Earth's surface. We haven't mapped them, and they're an unknown to us. We call them blind faults."

"And the equipment we're installing will check for movements in these blind faults?"

Tyler nodded furiously, his glasses slipping down his nose. He pushed them back, and that damn smile was back again. "That's it in a nutshell. We can't track the faults through traditional geologic studies. We need data from a permanent network of seismograph stations, and this installation will become the latest addition to the Montana Regional Seismic Network, which collates everything to become what is, in effect, an early warning system."

He sat back in his chair, his explanation complete, and Martin considered what he'd read in the essay he'd downloaded to his Kindle to bring with him. He should keep his mouth shut—people like Tyler wouldn't understand how his head worked—but he wasn't an idiot. He was able to understand way more than people gave him credit for. He hadn't received much of a formal education, but he'd worked damn hard to get a degree because he loved math, and his brain retained all kinds of information in a near perfect photographic way. He wanted Tyler to explain things to him using words of more than one syllable and maybe not with the hand gestures to demonstrate the theory. On the one hand, he could say nothing and have Tyler spend the entire week assuming Martin wasn't able to understand. On the other, he could just come out with it. After all, what did it matter? After this week, they would be done, and he'd leave Crooked Tree and head south. What did it hurt to have one person see evidence of his thought process?

He cleared his throat and dipped his gaze, unable to look Tyler in the face as he spoke.

"I read this thing last night that the network monitors seismicity along the northern Intermountain Seismic Belt in the Northern Rocky Mountains and into surrounding regions, producing records of ground movement at all the seismograph stations in the Montana Seismograph. That's right, isn't it?"

Tyler mouth fell open, and he shut it again. "You know that?"

"It was in an essay about interpreting waveforms." Martin shrugged as if it was nothing, but it was everything to give Tyler even the remotest idea he had an actual brain. Not only that, but that he was smart in his own way.

"You read an essay on interpreting waveforms?" Tyler blinked at him. "Waveforms." It appeared that was the important keyword here, but to Martin, at the end of the day, it was just math.

"I have the article on my Kindle. It didn't all make sense, not the technical definitions, but I think I got a feel for what we're doing here."

"Did you understand the waveforms?" Tyler pressed and sat forward in his chair, his eyes gleaming with unrestrained enthusiasm.

Of course he understood them. The crude rudimentary screen captures were a small part of what he imagined was unaccountable amounts of data. So much data it would take a lifetime to work through.

"The diagrams they used were easy enough to understand, but I know it's only part of the data."

"But it's a start, right? I have so much I can tell you about that."

Martin imagined him rubbing his hands in glee at the thought he could talk crazy earth science with the guy who'd said he wasn't a cowboy and just moved things.

"I need to be honest with you, though." Martin hesitated a moment. "I tend to recall things I've read, and a lot of it can go over my head, apart from math. I have a skill with math. I have an eidetic memory. At least that is what I think it is."

"Eidetic? So you read something and then remember the words?" Tyler sounded almost disappointed, which was a different reaction to the few others he'd told. They'd all wanted to put him on quiz shows or make them money in other ways, but Tyler was different. For a brief moment he'd been visibly dissatisfied at Martin's admission he was repeating information he'd read. Then he brightened. "That is *so* cool."

When they headed back up to the work area, Tyler chatted on about memory and knowledge, and not for one moment did he say he thought Martin's head was fucked up.

That was a first.

They began to dig, and it was backbreaking work, but it wasn't just Martin who dug. Tyler was happy to get down and dirty, and the two of them managed to move the earth by the end of day one. What was left was a large hole, four foot by six, and down five. Of course it would have been easier with some kind of excavator, but that hadn't been in the budget, or so Tyler explained. It was backbreaking but honest work. They left a box in the bottom of the hole, enough to step onto, so they could scramble out when they needed, but with legs and arms like jelly now, it was more of a drag and flop to the ground. They'd long since discarded their coats. Even though the air was cold, the sun had shone its best, and they were both hot from work.

They got into each other's spaces a lot, sharing water, accidentally bumping one another, and as the day went on, the awareness of Tyler being super close to him was a hell of a big thing. Martin didn't do enforced proximity; the thought of being stuck in this small space without a view of the sky and with another person next to him was enough for his throat to close up on a couple of occasions. He breathed through the panic attacks or excused himself for a break, and they'd actually made it through nearly the entire day, but by the time they were done, he was vibrating with feelings, the strongest of which was lust. Because as Tyler stripped off each layer as they grew hotter, more of him was exposed, and Martin couldn't fight the attraction.

Been too long since I've felt anything. Way too long.

All he could think was that this was dangerous, and he needed to fight the lust with every fiber of him.

Martin scraped the last of the mud onto his shovel and tipped it up and over the top of the hole and then patted the level so it was smooth.

"Tomorrow we need to place two vaults inside the space: one for the seismometer and one for the digitizer and battery. I was going to suggest today, but it's delicate work, and my limbs are like noodles. You ready to go?"

Martin nodded, sweat trickling down his face. He pulled up his shirt and wiped at his face, then tilted his head to the sky. The blue, cloudless, endless view was enough to make him catch his breath. When he glanced back, Tyler was staring at his belly, and he followed the gaze to where his shirt had caught on the undershirt and displayed a strip of flesh that really shouldn't have been causing Tyler to seem so dazed. He probably had something else on his mind and wasn't actually staring at Martin's body as if it were a puzzle to be solved.

"Sorry," Tyler apologized and checked out in a very deliberate way *anything* that wasn't Martin. The sky, rocks, even the clumps of mud that had rolled away from the site.

"What for?" Martin asked, confused about what it was that Tyler was apologizing for. The chance of the lust in Martin burning inside Tyler as well was unlikely, so it couldn't have been that. Only Tyler's tongue poked out and wet his lips, and he forced his hands into his jeans pockets.

"I'm going to be honest here," Tyler began. "You stretched, and then you looked up, and when you pulled your shirt, you looked… I need to stop talking."

Martin felt hot not just from the work but from the insidious creep of vulnerability mixed with that lust. He'd had enough of people saying shit to him to throw him off-balance, and he didn't want Tyler to be like them.

"Would it help if I said banana?" Martin murmured, and Tyler shook his head.

"I'm a grown man. I can…"

Martin moved around him to pick up the shovels, and Tyler made a noise that could only be identified as a groan. It sounded as if he was hurt, and Martin turned to face him, concerned, wanting to check him out. Only this put them very close, face-to-face, Tyler pressed against the wall of soil and Martin so near that if they leaned in a little more, they could kiss.

"Martin, would it be…?" He took his hands from his pockets and used his index finger to push an errant curl from Martin's face. Then he moved slowly, so slowly that Martin had every chance to step away, but he didn't. He was frozen in place, and the kiss when it came was so gentle, so damn soft, that Martin could have cried. The lust was gone, replaced by a need for someone to care about him, and that was dangerous. He pulled back, confused by how he felt, and Tyler smiled.

"I've wanted to do that all day; do I need to apologize?" he asked. "I mean, I don't technically employ you. You're just getting expenses, and you're here on—"

Martin pressed an answering kiss to Tyler's lips, mostly to stop him from talking, but also because he wanted one small taste before he put an end to this.

"That makes us even," he said. "Now, let's get out of here."

Martin didn't have to imagine the relief that passed over Tyler's face.

Tyler stood on the box, and it wobbled, but he managed to scramble out when Martin gave him a helping hand on his ass. An ass, which was hard and muscled, and he was *so* not thinking about that right now. He passed up the tools, and then it was his turn to climb out. He used the box himself, but it wasn't stable and would need to be wedged in place for the next day. Still, he managed to get halfway up before it slid away, and Tyler was there with his hand extended to help Martin out. He used his body weight to support the simple climb and toppled onto his back, Martin sprawling over him. For a second they lay there, belly to groin, so close that Martin could see the green flecks in

Tyler's hazel eyes. Tyler gripped his arms, but whether it was to push Martin away or pull him closer, Martin couldn't tell.

The thought of kissing, of touching, spooked Martin, and he heaved himself up and ended on his back next to Tyler. That had been a weird moment, but Martin wasn't stupid. He'd seen interest in Tyler's expression, and coupled with the kiss was more proof that something was going on in Tyler's head.

I kissed him back.

I liked it.

I want more, even if I can't have it.

"We won't be able to move tomorrow," Tyler said with a groan, rolling onto his knees and standing. Martin followed suit. Then with tarpaulins pulled over everything, they headed downhill. Neither mentioned the couple of awkward moments, and between them, they organized heating the contents of a vacuum-packed stew and used the small stove to boil potatoes. Right now, the potatoes were fresh. It would be a few days before they moved on to canned food, and that was only if they needed to stay for calibration of the instruments if anything went wrong.

"If you need to charge your Kindle, I have a solar charger," Tyler announced just as Martin had taken a mouthful of beef. He chewed and swallowed; his Kindle was his escape, and he'd brought chargers and hoped to have used the small generator, but of course the power of the sun didn't cost them valuable fuel.

"Thank you."

Tyler poked at the fire with a stick, and Martin knew there were going to be more questions. "So you read a lot, then?"

"All the time."

"And you recall all of it."

"Mostly."

"Your head…" Tyler tapped his temple. "It must be so full of all the good things and the bad."

Too full. Of useless information, of things that he wanted to keep forever, and others that he'd never wanted to think about again. The fact that Tyler understood that made him edgy. He didn't like the direction of this conversation, and avoidance was called for.

"Why now for the monitoring station out here on Crooked Tree? The rest of the units in the network have been installed a lot longer." He was changing the subject and he knew it.

Tyler took the bait and rambled on for a long time about budgets and proposals. Not once did Martin think to say *banana* because listening to Tyler talk and laugh was his new drug, and he was slowly becoming addicted.

They didn't mention the kisses. They didn't act on anything that had passed between them, and that was fine by Martin. The last thing he needed in his life right now was pity sex with a desperate man who was in the middle of nowhere and who had an itch to scratch.

THE NIGHTMARES VISITED THAT NIGHT.

Martin knew they would.

Inevitably they ended in fire and tasted of pain and regret, and when he woke, he was exhausted, edgy, and filled with a familiar self-hatred.

So much for peace and calm with a man who actually seemed to want to know him.

For the longest time he sat on his cot, head bowed, following all the advice he'd been given in order to be able to center himself. He was on a hair-trigger, and it would take every single ounce of self-control for him to interact with the world today. These days happened, but back in Vermont, he would open the coffee shop, stay behind the counter, do his work, then quietly shut the place before hiding on the roof. It didn't matter if it was raining or freezing or the sun baked him, he'd lay flat on his back and stare.

Today they were working on the installation satellite dish and GPS array.

All he had to do was focus. Get through the day. Not lose his shit.

Easy.

Chapter Nine

BY THE END OF THEIR THIRD DAY, TYLER DECIDED THAT Martin was a nice guy. Not that he hadn't thought that from that first grocery delivery or the rock-carrying incident. Things happened that kept making Tyler want to smile, which then morphed into the desire to grab Martin and kiss him all kinds of inappropriately.

Yep. Kiss. Again.

Like when Martin had stood in that excavation and wiped his face, then tilted his head toward the sun. Tyler had never seen anything so perfect, with damp curls escaping from the thin tie that held back the majority of his mahogany hair. Add in the glimpse of the skin of his belly, and Tyler was gone. Then he'd fucked it up when Martin had caught him staring, compounded by the nonsense that had fallen out of his mouth.

The kiss he'd thrown at Martin had been clumsy and ill-timed, but from his point of view, it had also been one of the most perfect first kisses he'd ever experienced. Then Martin had kissed him back, but was that just to even the playing field, or had it actually meant something?

Then there was the fact that Martin remembered everything he read. Tyler had never met anyone with a true eidetic memory, and the concept fascinated him, but the last thing he wanted to do was ask questions from a scientific point of view. That would be like treating Martin as if he was a bug under a microscope. Today he'd been quiet and blamed it on not sleeping. There was tension in him that even the least observant person could've spotted, in the way he walked and worked and in the fact that answers to questions were even more monosyllabic than usual.

They'd worked hard, the concrete was dry, ceramic tiles in place, and in the next couple of days they would be able to complete both vaults and fill in the spaces between them. At the moment it was about the satellite dish, which ordinarily was one of the most straightforward tasks to do. Dig a hole, install wiring, get the thing to stand up.

It wouldn't stay at the right angle, a combination of soil issues, rock placement, and general bad luck.

"Just take it slower," Tyler explained, balancing the wire as Martin moved the array.

"I am."

"Not slow enough, one inch, no more."

Martin was growing tenser at each failure to get the solar panel to stay in the position they needed it to be. At first, Tyler had laughed off the fact that the expensive equipment wouldn't connect to the right wires, but Martin didn't seem that impressed with his attempt to diffuse the situation. If anything, he was taking things personally, and Tyler got the feeling he was spoiling for a fight. Then as Martin tried for another go, his movements became shaky, and Tyler placed a hand over his to stop him.

"Leave it, Martin. I've got it."

Martin stared at him. "I can do this."

"I know you can, but this is expensive equipment, and I don't want you going all Hulk on it," he was teasing, but Martin's expression turned hard, and he stepped back.

"I'm fucking it up."

"No, you just need to appreciate that this is—"

"Understood," he snapped, then strode down the hill, his hands in fists at his sides.

Tyler took a few moments to make sure everything was secure and then jogged after him. He felt as if he owed Martin an apology or at least a moment where he listened to Martin's reasons for walking off and for them to come to a solution. There was no sign of him at the camp, but a glimpse of denim confirmed he was back in what Tyler thought of as Martin's thinking spot. Only this time he wasn't sitting on top of the drop stone; he was on the ground next to it, his legs drawn up, his arms wrapped around them, and his face tilted to the sky.

"You know we'll get it to work eventually," Tyler offered lamely, and Martin glanced at him, looking exhausted. Forget apologies or sane conversations about procedure. All Tyler wanted to do was go to his knees next to him and hug him.

That would be seriously crossing the lines.

"I just need a minute," Martin murmured.

Sometimes Tyler did stupid things, like asking questions when he shouldn't or prodding at people who clearly wanted to be left alone. With hindsight, he should have walked away and left Martin to chill for a few minutes, but no, he didn't want Martin stressing over things that could be easily cleared up, so in his infinite wisdom, he proceeded to poke the bear.

"Was it because I kissed you yesterday?"

"No."

"Because you kissed me back, but if I overstepped—"

"Go away."

Tyler should have taken the hint then, but no, he went after Martin even more. If it wasn't the kiss, then what was it exactly?

"What happened up there? You looked as if you were going to throw the panel off a cliff."

Martin shot him a glance that spoke volumes, but Tyler ignored him and pressed ahead.

"It's not an issue. That wiring is notoriously hard to get right, and it's my fault." He wanted to lower the angst going on here, so to add insult to injury, he inserted a joke. "I should have given you the manual so you could read about the installation. Then you'd remember the procedure with the super expensive government equipment." He let out a soft laugh at his own lame joke.

This time Martin looked right at him. "Seriously, you went *there*?"

"What do you mean? I was only joking. It doesn't—"

"Fuck you," Martin snapped, and he stood in angry jerky motions. "I know I'm shit, but don't you dare think that reading some manual will instantly make me fucking perfect. I'm allowed to get things wrong. It's okay to make mistakes." With every statement, he moved closer to Tyler, and even though he thought

Martin wouldn't hurt him, there was genuine temper in his expression. What the hell had happened? Was this some kind of breakdown?

"Of course it's okay, Martin. Can you just—"

Martin shoved past him, "I said I need ten fucking minutes. That's all I asked for."

"Martin, stop being so melodramatic—"

"Jesus!" Martin snapped and stalked away.

Tyler watched him go, right through the camp and into the trees beyond. His first instinct was to follow, but there was something seriously wrong here, and it was all his fault. He kicked the drop stone, something he regretted immediately and then hobbled away and limped back up the hill to the site with a view to getting things done.

Martin came back after ten minutes, but in the way of men when the atmosphere was shit, they went about what they were doing in silence until finally the satellite dish was situated. The solar panel was less trouble to put in place, and when the time came when they couldn't do any more until the concrete had dried, they'd actually achieved the list of things that Tyler had in his head for today.

"Okay if I get a shower?" Martin asked, waited for Tyler to nod, then disappeared into their bathroom tent, lugging a huge container of spring water. Tyler tried not to think about Martin in there, naked, under the water, and instead focused on whatever had happened to get inside Martin's head and have him freaked out for most of the day.

"It must have been me. I shouldn't even be allowed out among normal people," Tyler berated himself quietly, then took one of the cloth bags he'd stuffed into his duffle and stalked up the hill, toward the point where the stream came out of the mountainside after its underground journey. He collected as much gravel as he could carry, then tied the top. That was for the next spare minute he had, for the downtime when he came back down to the camp, Martin's tent was zipped up. Dinner wouldn't be for a while, he had fucked up being in charge of this installation, and now Martin was in hiding, but instead of thinking about any of that, Tyler set about writing up notes about the day in his journal.

He got as far as putting the date at the top of the page when Martin stepped out of his tent and crossed the campsite to stand next to him.

"I owe you an apology," he murmured. "Sorry."

Tyler scrambled to stand. "No, I'm sorry too. I was joking, but I was also serious, and I was using the joking to cover up the fact that this is expensive equipment that I am responsible for, and today you've been on edge, and I should have asked you what was wrong way before you got into a personal fight with the satellite dish because that would have been good management, but then I worried about the kiss because I wanted to kiss you, and I'd like to kiss you again, but I get that—"

"I had a shit night's sleep," Martin interrupted. "Too many memories, too much everything."

"Do you want to talk about it?"

Martin barked a laugh, and it sounded hollow and pained. "If I talked to you about all the crap in my head, you'd run back to the ranch in an instant."

That was some statement weighed down with emotion, almost as if Martin was daring Tyler to ask him questions.

"We're stuck here together for a few days. I can be a

friend," Tyler suggested. He was treading in untested waters. His experience with emotions was limited by the fact that he spent most of his life with his head in a book or out in isolation, just him and his rocks. Something heavy was going on with Martin, and what did Tyler really know about him? Other than he'd carried rocks in a very sexy way. Or that he'd packed away groceries and had the strong legs of a runner and the gentle hands of an artist. Although the satellite dish might argue that Martin wasn't gentle, but that was just how Tyler saw him. Then there were his eyes, which were chips of green ice, and when he smiled, he was the sexiest man Tyler had ever seen.

Maybe he wanted to be more than a friend, but Martin didn't need to know that.

"Just a friend," Tyler repeated. "If you want to talk."

"Not tonight," Martin said, and that was the end of the conversation.

Dinner was quiet but companionable, and when they went to their individual tents, the events of today had passed by. Or at least, they'd been hidden away.

That was enough for now.

Chapter Ten

"THIS IS THE TRILLIUM SEISMOMETER," TYLER announced and lifted something from a box with utmost care. It was as if he was handling a newborn baby with a gentle but firm hold. "This is what actually picks up the movements." He scooted forward on his elbows just a few inches and then maneuvered it into place, setting it down gently on the ceramic tile and then referring to his iPad. Martin stayed absolutely quiet, sitting cross-legged on the grass and waiting to help if he was needed. This was day five now, and after fighting the foil insulation and deciding that it was the work of the devil, they were at the point where they were ready to bury the equipment in the seismometer vault. They still had the other vault with the power and extra parts to do, but the most crucial step was happening now.

Tyler muttered to himself as he stared at the iPad, tutting, sighing, smiling, and finally scooting back from the edge.

"Okay, now the sand. Slowly. We'll do a little at a time and take care not to nudge the monitor. Watch how

I do this." Martin moved forward, with his own cup of sand, and watched as Tyler demonstrated how the sand needed to go in. There was a lot of sand and a big hole, but it didn't seem as if the task was a throw-it-in-and-go kind of job.

It took them at least two hours, both of them on their bellies for some of it and quiet with concentration. Only when the first bag of sand was in over the seismometer did Tyler seem to loosen up. He checked readouts on his iPad, and then with a triumphant and very loud "aha!" he rolled onto his back and did some kind of weird hand-waving-dancing on the ground thing.

There was something about the super intelligent geologist squirming on the ground, which made Martin smile, and it was that expression Tyler saw when he turned to face him.

"It's a thing, you know," Tyler explained, "a patented geologist dance." He patted the ground next to him. "You need to do it too; otherwise the magic seismometer won't work."

Martin lay on the ground. "You're saying you control magic."

"Of course. Now wave your hands as if no one is watching."

"Apart from you," Martin said dryly but waved his hands in an approximation of Tyler's geologist dance.

Tyler rolled onto his elbows to watch him, and his gaze was heated. "You're easy to watch," he said.

Martin digested that comment, which when he unpacked it in his head sounded like flirting. He decided to be honest with Tyler because confusion was his go-to place right now. He wasn't ready to form any kind of attachment. He wasn't prepared to let anyone in and show them all the horrors in his head, or allow them to divert him from continuing to pay for his sins. "I don't know what to say back to that."

"Don't you ever... I mean... with other guys. Or girls. I'm not one to jump to conclusions..." This time he stopped talking all by himself, and he didn't need Martin to say banana at all.

"My life is complicated." *It's a mess.*

"So you don't kiss? I mean, I'd like to kiss you again if that was okay with you?"

"Let's get the sand done first," Martin hedged because to admit he wanted to kiss Tyler now was to open himself up to more nightmares tonight. He had to keep a lid on his emotions; otherwise they might just tear him apart.

"If I have to," Tyler groused but was soon back in the zone.

By the time they inserted insulation to plug the space and then temporarily sealed the lid, Tyler seemed a long way from thinking about kissing. That suited Martin just fine.

They moved to the other compartment, which housed the batteries and various pieces of monitoring equipment, and then put a temporary seal on that as well.

"That's all we can do until we have a minimum of forty-eight hours of reports from the equipment," Tyler said as he patted the lid of the second vault.

"What if it's wrong? What if it doesn't work?"

"Then we'd need to take all the sand out, run diagnostics. In fact let's not think about that." His stomach rumbled, and he patted his belly. "I seriously need food, and I swear there was some chicken dish that Sam was excited about giving to us." They headed back down to camp, but it had begun to rain, the path slick and treacherous. Martin stumbled a couple of times, and ahead of him, Tyler wasn't having much better luck; they were both wearing hiking boots, but the descent was steep.

Tyler slid on a flat stone, his hands wind-milling, and he began to topple, head first into a pile of boulders. Thinking quickly, Martin put himself between Tyler and the stones, and the weight of Tyler falling back pushed him heavily into the immovable force. The impact hurt. He let out a yelp, and Tyler squirmed off him in an instant.

"Shit, Martin," He helped Martin up, checking for wounds, but all Martin would be left with was bruises. Nothing was broken. "Why did you do that?"

"We don't want the scientist to go head first into rocks," Martin explained and then brushed off any more concern, carefully picking his way down to the level ground, with Tyler hovering at his side.

"I need to look at your ribs. That was a heavy fall."

"No, you don't. I'm fine. Do your thing, and I'll fix dinner."

The dish for tonight was Chicken Provençal, which, according to the label Sam had placed on it, was Mediterranean. Whatever it was, it tasted delicious, and this was unlike any kind of camping Martin could recall.

He cleared everything away and left Tyler scribbling furiously with the pen on his iPad, making notes about the installation and adding the initial data analysis, which he didn't seem worried by, so Martin assumed it was all okay. He took some standard pain meds because his left arm had started to ache, and then went over to the drop rock, which had become his favorite place to sit. This time he'd brought a blanket, and he spread it out on the ground. The blackness of the night was all-consuming, trees mere smudges, and the sound of the water over pebbles lulled him into relaxing. He sensed when Tyler joined him, knew it was inevitable, and scooted over when he sat on the blanket and lay down.

"Are we geologist-dancing again?" Tyler asked quietly.

"No, I'm just watching the sky."

"Counting the stars?"

"Some."

"I don't know constellations that well, I look at what's under my feet, not the sky so much, even though most of what we have on earth has come from out there." He wriggled closer to Martin. "I can't name a single star up there."

"I can, but I don't think of their names. I just think it's beautiful and that whether it's night or day, the stars are always there."

Tyler sighed softly.

"Thank you for not letting me split my head open," Tyler said.

"You're welcome."

Silence again, but it wasn't uncomfortable. Then Tyler ruined it all by talking.

"About that kiss," he said and then stopped as if he wasn't ready to say anymore.

Martin should say something, explain his past, maybe even tell Tyler his real name, but he didn't want to do any of that. He didn't want to mess up right now; he just wanted a kiss under the stars.

He turned onto his side and supported his weight on one elbow. "You don't know me well enough to really want to kiss me. It's just proximity, is all." He waited for Tyler to roll out the lines, the ones that said he knew enough and could they get on with kissing?

Tyler chuckled. "No. I don't. I still want to kiss you though, just to feel you, on a purely experimental basis." He reached up and collected one of Martin's curls with his fingers, tugging on it slightly and then pushing it behind his ear. "When you do an experiment, you need a hypothesis. My hypothesis is that kissing you will be incendiary. Now I need a method to prove it."

Tyler carded his fingers into Martin's hair and pulled him down slowly until they were nothing more than a breath apart. Then they kissed, Martin slanting his head, Tyler deepening the kiss, his other hand gripping Martin's arm. This wasn't like any other kiss Martin had ever had, not like the fumbling kisses he'd shared with Levi when he was a kid and nothing like the kisses he'd shared on the odd occasion he'd hooked up. This was kissing for the sake of kissing, and their tongues tangled lazily. He was so hard, had been since the moment Tyler had lain down next to him, the expectation of this kiss enough to send blood rushing south. When they separated, for a moment Martin thought Tyler was going to call a stop to this, but he didn't.

He cradled Martin's face, and then they were kissing again. Poised on that delicious edge where he was so turned on but couldn't do anything about it. He deepened the kiss and moved subtly closer, his erection just against Tyler's thigh. With his free hand, he traced a path down Tyler's chest and slid in to find any bare skin he could. He just wanted to touch, to feel his way around this intriguing man's body. Tyler shuddered beneath him as Martin's fingertips pushed under the belt of his jeans, and in a smooth motion, he rolled them both and settled between Martin's spread legs.

"You can't," Tyler muttered and kissed Martin again, capturing Martin's hands and holding them loosely.

Martin didn't like to be held down and wriggled on instinct, but that wasn't enough to stop the kiss, and he focused hard on the kiss and not on the feeling of being trapped.

Tyler stilled and broke the kiss. "What's wrong?" he whispered.

Martin closed his eyes. What a fucking loser that he couldn't bear having the weight of someone on him. "Keep going," he muttered through gritted teeth, forcing himself to relax, and then Tyler moved up and away, sitting cross-legged on the blanket.

"I want to, but I won't," he summarized. "Something is wrong, and we can talk about it if you want? Or not."

Martin had two options, and he knew it. He could either get up and walk away, or he could be honest. He was still hard, still wanted to kiss, wanted more than that. Needed it. He had no option, really.

"I don't like to be held down, and if that is a deal breaker—" He let out a yelp as Tyler lay down and pulled him until Martin was sprawled over Tyler like a blanket.

"Good thing I love being held down," Tyler explained. "Lie between my legs and hold my hands."

Martin did as he was told, on auto-pilot, and laced his fingers with Tyler's. Like this, he could feel how hard

Tyler was, and that just made things worse. "Now, press down and hold me still and kiss me."

When they kissed this time with Tyler arching up against *him*, it was the most intense feeling of being in control, and it was intoxicating. He could have so much of this in the time they had here, just kissing and connecting on a level he hadn't imagined he could ever find. Without even realizing, he released his hold on Tyler, and between them, they pushed at clothes until finally, blessedly, their cocks slid against each other, and for Martin, it was the end of being able to think rationally. He raised his hips, unable to do much at this angle, and let Tyler get them off; he was mindless with lust, with need, his orgasm right there just out of reach. Somehow they found a rhythm.

"You're beautiful," Tyler breathed into the kiss, and then he was arching, coming hard, and he couldn't know that his words had ruined everything for Martin.

There was nothing beautiful about him, and it was wrong for Tyler to think so.

Arousal gone, he rolled off Tyler, who tried to grab him playfully, only stopping when Martin stumbled back from him. That single word. *Beautiful.*

"I'm not," he stuttered in horror.

He tripped back over himself, falling to his ass and clambering back in an instant. In the moon's glow, Tyler sat and watched him

"Martin?"

"You're wrong," Martin snapped and headed for his tent, vanishing inside and closing the entrance. The zipper stuck, and he yanked at it until finally it gave, and then curled into a ball of misery on his cot.

I'm not beautiful.

Chapter Eleven

Tyler went from sated to alert in an instant. He didn't know what had happened, but somehow the word *beautiful* had triggered Martin in some way. He'd been one hundred percent into it, Tyler was sure of it, but now he'd run, and Tyler didn't know what to do next.

He'd never seen this before.

He tucked himself away, wrinkling his nose at the cold wetness, and then pulled up his jeans before heading directly to Martin's tent.

"Martin?" He couldn't exactly knock on a tent, but he called soft and low and tapped the upright. "Are you okay?"

Silence.

"Martin?"

Still nothing, and Tyler wasn't going to push things by going in and demanding to know what had happened. He'd gotten the sense that what they'd just done had been hard for Martin, and all he wanted to do was hug him and listen to him talk so he could help. That clearly wasn't happening tonight.

"I'll be here if you need me," he said softly, then wondered what the hell to do next. At first, he decided he had sex-brain, and that explained why he wandered aimlessly up to the installation, then back down again. Until finally, he wrapped himself in his coat against the swiftly cooling night air, then sat for a while on the drop rock and listened to the water. It was obvious what he was *really* doing: he was waiting for Martin to come out of his tent. When it passed ten p.m. and nothing happened, he resigned himself to going to bed, taking his time, writing up notes, or at least pretending to write up notes, all the while watching Martin's tent. There was no light in there, no sound of movement, and if he knew Martin better, then maybe he'd just be able to go over there and demand to talk to him.

But he didn't. They'd known each other for a very short time, he'd gotten off against him in the dark, a fumbled, desperate match of hands and cocks. Martin was quiet, focused, shy, but other than that, what did Tyler know about the man who'd gotten under his skin? Nothing. He checked in with Crooked Tree with the sat-phone, and then he had nothing left to work on, which meant he could sit and stare at Martin's tent.

He was almost in bed, literally zipping up his sleeping bag when he heard the shouting. It sounded like an argument, yelling, cursing, and he was up and out of bed in an instant, forcing his legs into pants and wondering why he'd refused to bring a rifle as everyone had wanted him to. Not that he would have used it—he hated weapons—but just waving it around could've been a good thing. All he had was a tranquilizer gun, which was like a simple tube and meant to be used in case of emergencies with wild animals. Any self-respecting bad guy would take one look at the thing and laugh Tyler out of town. He pocketed it anyway and grabbed a flashlight. Then he stepped out into the darkness and turned in a full circle, letting the beam of the flashlight find every nook and cranny.

Only after he took his bearings did he realize the shouting was coming from Martin's tent and had actually become less shouting and more cursing. And sobbing? Martin was in there crying? Tyler didn't stop to think, and the zipper was undone, leaving the entrance to Martin's tent gaping, as he stepped in.

The punch knocked him on his ass, flat to the ground, the flashlight spinning away from him, coming to rest by the cot and casting a wide glow. A snarling Martin sat on Tyler and held him flat, but in the soft light, Tyler could see it wasn't actually Martin there. It *was* Martin, but his eyes were glazed and his movements jerky and uncoordinated. He was in the middle of a nightmare, sleepwalking, a hole dug into the floor of his tent, his entire front covered in mud, and his eyes wide with fear.

"Martin, it's me, Tyler. You remember me. I burn bacon." He kept talking with a low voice. "I'm the idiot geologist, and you probably need to wake up because you're going to hurt yourself. Why are you covered in mud? What have you been doing? Come on, Martin, wake up for me."

He knew that conventional wisdom suggested he shouldn't wake him up, but Martin was heavy, and it hurt, and when light flashed off a trowel in Martin's belt, Tyler knew this had to come to a stop. He bucked up to get Martin off, and Martin rolled back, coming to a crouch, and *fuck*, the trowel was in his hand, held up like a weapon. He advanced on Tyler, murderous intent in his expression.

Tyler was on his feet in an instant, poised to get the fuck out of the tent. "Wake up!" he shouted and hurled the nearest thing he could find, a shoe, right at Martin's chest. In an instant, Martin appeared to snap out of the nightmare, his features relaxing, his eyes clearing, and then there was shock on his face as he stared, horrified at the trowel, and he let it slip to the ground, cursing loudly. He stumbled back until his legs hit the cot, and then he sat heavily and buried his face in his hands. After a while, as his breathing slowed, he pulled his hands away and examined them as if it was the first time he'd seen them, picking at mud ingrained in his nails.

"Shit," he said with feeling.

Tyler could've backed away, gone to his own tent, not even tried to get involved here. A man was entitled to privacy, but when he glanced up at Tyler and his eyes were wet with tears, Tyler acted on instinct and sat next to him. He put an arm over Martin's shoulders and squeezed a little.

"It was just a nightmare," Tyler said encouragingly, as if that would make it all better.

Martin cleared his throat and then coughed. He was cold and began to shiver. Tyler pulled a blanket around him before zipping up the tent and shutting them inside. Martin shuffled uncomfortably and threw a worried look at the tent entrance, but he didn't say anything.

Tyler joined Martin again, and stole one of the other blankets to wrap around himself.

"You want to talk about it?"

Martin laughed humorlessly and shook his head.

"We still have to work together," he said as if that explained everything.

"I heard some words," Tyler said. "I can make my own assumptions. I heard 'no.' Actually a lot of 'no's' and 'get out,' and the name Xander."

Martin shuddered and scrubbed at his eyes. "Xander," he repeated.

"Was this all my fault? I know this isn't about me, but if I did something I shouldn't, then please tell me what I can do to fix it."

Martin was deathly quiet for a long time, but for once, Tyler managed to stop himself from talking and instead waited for Martin to talk.

"He used to call me beautiful." Martin's voice was raw, probably from the shouting. "Xander did, I mean."

"Is he an ex?"

"God no. But he was the first person who hurt me. Had sex with me."

Tyler picked up on the inflection of the words immediately. Had sex *with* me.

"Okay…" Tyler left it open so that Martin could either talk to him or not. Something awful lived in his nightmares, and it was up to Martin whether or not he wanted to share.

"I'm heading south after this," Martin murmured, and Tyler strained to hear. "I can't stay at Crooked Tree, so I'm heading south, getting as far away from here as possible."

Wait. Was the pain that Martin was experiencing due to something at Crooked Tree? Had they hurt him? They'd all seemed kind of cool, even Nate with his no-drones obsession.

"Did something happen at the ranch? Is that where Xander is?"

Martin flinched at the name, then shook his head. "No. Crooked Tree has good people there. Family. Real family."

None of this was making sense, and Tyler thought maybe they should stop talking now and leave everything to be examined in the light of day. Or not. Whatever Martin decided.

"Do you have a family?" Martin asked abruptly and stared right at Tyler.

"Mom, Dad, a younger sister, Siobhan." He waited for more questions, but when none came, he pressed on. "Mom and Dad are professors at Seattle University. My sister is married to a journalist and has three children who keep her busy. She's also a graphic artist, so she works from home. You don't need to know all that."

"I want to know. Tell me more."

"Siobhan is four years younger than me, and she's tiny, like she comes up to my chest, but she has three boys and keeps them in line with this look she has perfected. She kind of stares at them, and I've seen it in action when her youngest, Petey, stole cookies, and his face was covered in chocolate, like he couldn't have been more than five, and he was standing there with the evidence on his face, denying it all. She just gave him this stare, and he unraveled in about ten seconds. She got all the confident genes, but I ended up with my dad's love of geology and the nerdy brain with it."

"They sound cool."

"Yep, and her kids are just as confident. Petey, he's seven now, Lewis ten, and the oldest is Jamie."

A cloud settled over Martin's face, and the relaxed state he'd been slipping into disappeared in an instant.

"I have something else to tell you," he whispered. "My real name isn't Martin."

"What do you mean?"

"My real name is Jamie."

His real name? What the hell?

Chapter Twelve

ALL MARTIN COULD THINK WAS WHY IN THE NAME OF all that's holy had he said that?

Because it doesn't matter anymore. Because who the hell cares if I'm Jamie fucking Crane or Martin scared-as-shit Graves.

Waking up from the night terror, with that damn trowel in his hand, crouched ready to fight, with blood lust in his veins, all he'd seen in front of him was Xander Walden. Gray hair to his shoulders, a tangled beard, stinking of beer, he'd been the stuff of childhood nightmares. A close friend of his dad's, he'd joined them in the compound before Martin could remember. Another member of the group who believed anarchy would allow them to make America great, he was one of four men who'd been his entire young life.

"Jamie? That's a good name. Strong," Tyler said and pulled the blanket he'd borrowed closer around him in a metaphoric shield against Martin. Not that he needed it, because Martin couldn't hurt anyone, not even in a nightmare. *Could he?* "But I like Martin more for you."

"Jamie died a long time ago, killed off in a car

accident or a murder. I don't know how he actually died, but the moment it happened, I became Martin."

"Was this a witness protection thing?"

Martin nodded because that was as close a description as he could get. What had happened was that he'd taken every single dollar his dad had stashed, all the gold he'd hoarded, what there was of it, and he'd bought himself a new life. The day the group had tried to kill Justin and Adam and it had all gone to shit was the day he'd grown a pair and left.

He'd called the cops and run. Bought a new identity, tried to build something for himself, and stayed terrified his dad would find him, until the day Justin had walked into the coffee shop and said in no uncertain terms that David Crane was dead.

"I won't say anything to anyone," Tyler insisted. The flashlight turned itself off, plunging the tent into darkness, and for a moment Martin's chest tightened. The dark didn't scare him. What scared him was the fact he was sitting here and he wanted to tell Tyler everything.

He didn't even really know the man.

Yeah, I do know him. I know enough. He's one of the good guys, and I need that. In fact, right now, the darkness invited confidences, and he wanted to talk. *Really* wanted to talk.

"I was ten, the first time Xander got me alone and… hurt me."

Next to him Tyler let out a low curse.

"Ten."

"Uh-huh. I didn't know anything to stop him. I didn't stop him until I was thirteen. We'd moved outside a little town in rural Ohio, and Xander didn't come with us. It was just me and my dad for a while. I didn't hate my dad, even though I knew he was a figure who should be loathed, because I didn't know any different. I was having alone time with a man who was my moral compass, for what it was worth. Does that make any sense?"

"Absolute sense. You were a kid, and you didn't know better."

"Yeah, I guess. There was this boy whom I met at the river. Levi was his name, and he was funny. You know, right to the bone, he was funny, and he had these eyes that sparkled the same as when the sun hits the water. He was good. We kissed, and for a short time I imagined everything could be perfect, that it would be okay. I'd found my sunshine, and I could move on from the way we lived, scratching and stealing and hurting people. Only, Xander came to find us, had this job he wanted to do with my dad, and I refused to leave, told them I'd fallen for a boy. You can imagine how that went down with men who thought *real* men couldn't be gay."

Tyler tensed next to him, and Martin considered that maybe he could leave the rest of the story for Tyler to fill in himself. But that was the coward's way out.

"The cops found Levi's body face down in the water the day after Xander arrived. I don't know if it was Xander who killed him or maybe my dad, but it didn't matter. My world was black and white again, and I left with them. But you know what? I kept a knife, and I told Xander outright I would fuck him over if he came near me. He never touched me again. But…"

The tears that had threatened and choked his throat, collected in his eyes and burned hot trails down his face.

Tyler was so quiet, but he had reached out and laced his hand with Martin's and hadn't left.

Martin sniffed back some tears, feeling a hundred kinds of broken and pathetic. The next part wasn't his story to tell in detail; Justin and Adam deserved their privacy and their lives.

"Because he couldn't hurt *me*, he started to hurt other kids. There were two that we found... when he and my dad and the others left them for dead, I took what I could find, and I ran and became Martin Graves. I worked in a coffee shop, kept my head down, faked school results, attended night school for a degree, all under this new name. I was going to make a difference, but somehow everything kept pulling me down. And tonight when you called me beautiful, it was a memory that forced its way back into my head, and I didn't want it there, because..." He stopped.

"Because?" Tyler prompted and squeezed his hand.

"What we did, what I had with you there, was the most normal, physical thing I've ever done, and I don't want his name anywhere near what short thing I could have with you. Counseling showed me that I deserved more, that I'd been a helpless kid and couldn't have changed my own life without help."

"That's true," Tyler said.

"After I got away from them, I lived for a long time thinking I was going to die, and when I didn't have that fear anymore, it was as if I'd lost the will to carry on, and I messed up, and then the place I worked at burned to the ground and took everything I owned with it. How fucking stupid is that?"

"It's not stupid," Tyler defended.

Martin bowed his head. "I'm so tired."

"You should sleep; maybe now the nightmare will leave you alone. Tomorrow we'll move the tent to a new spot so no one falls into the hole. Maybe tomorrow we can go looking for gold in the stream."

"There's gold here?"

"Probably a few flakes, so that's something to look forward to, right?"

Martin swung his legs up and slid to one side of the cot. The thing was bigger than the average cot, but to fit two grown men on it was going to be a squeeze, but if he scooted over as far as he could, then Tyler could hold him for a little while. "There's room for you."

"You need me to stay?"

Need? Maybe it was need, but right now, he couldn't put a label on how he felt. "I want," he said instead.

So curled up together in twisted blankets they lay still, and he waited until Tyler's breathing settled into a regular heavy rhythm before he let himself sleep.

And he hoped to hell the nightmare stayed away.

WHEN MARTIN WOKE, Tyler was gone, and for a few brief moments, the awful memories of what he'd said and done last night washed over him. No wonder Tyler had left; he'd probably gotten straight into the Jeep and headed back to the ranch.

"Coffee?" Tyler's voice startled him, and when Martin moved to face him, Tyler was crouched by the side of the cot holding out a mug. "Also I'm cooking the last of the bacon. You want some?"

"Thank you." Martin couldn't meet Tyler's gaze until Tyler placed his finger under Martin's chin and encouraged him to look up.

"I promise I will never tell another soul what you told me last night."

"Okay."

"Actually, have you ever heard of Geologist/Assistant privilege?"

"What?"

"It's where anything said on a camp stays on the camp and is never revealed. Like fight club, only for nerds."

"You just made that up," Martin accused, although his heart felt suddenly lighter at the words.

Tyler did something with his fingers, made an oval with them, and tapped himself on the head. "Geologist's promise."

Then he grinned and left, muttering something about burned bacon and lazy assistants.

And for the longest time ever, Martin found himself smiling at absolutely nothing.

Chapter Thirteen

TYLER POKED AT THE BACON, WAITED FOR MARTIN TO arrive at the fire, and hoped and prayed that everything wasn't fucked up. When he'd woken this morning, with Martin pressed hard against him, he'd ached in every muscle. The cot wasn't big enough for them both, but even though he'd woken a couple of times in the night, there was no way he would have moved. Martin slept, and the nightmares didn't chase into his sleep, so for that Tyler felt as if he was doing a good thing.

So what if his back ached now? Who cared about a little backache?

What he didn't want now was for what happened to change what they had between them. The fragile attraction, the interest, and now the shared knowledge could be enough for Martin to want to go back to Crooked Tree. Tyler had already decided that if Martin wanted the Jeep to return, then he would say yes. Nate could always bring it back to collect him when the work here was done if needed. Not that he wanted Martin to go. Actually that was the last thing he wanted. Martin was cool and new, and it could be fun here.

Remember his past, remember he's still healing from that. Stop being so fucking selfish.

Tyler pushed down his inner voice, reminding himself that he was willing to let Martin take the Jeep. Thing was, by the time Martin came out of the bathroom tent, looking as if he'd washed up and smoothed his curls with water, Tyler had all this pent-up energy and blurted out the first thing he thought of.

"You can take the Jeep if you want to go today."

Martin stopped in his steps and frowned. "You want me to leave? I get that, I guess, but I can call Nate, and he can collect me. I'm not leaving you here without a vehicle." He stepped closer and held out a hand. "Thank you for last night, for listening, for saying you'll keep my secrets."

Tyler took his hand, but instead of shaking it, he used it to tug Martin into a hug. "I never said I wanted you to go. The last thing I want is for you to leave. But if you need space, or you need to go, I'll understand."

Martin hugged him back, then stepped away and poked at the bacon on the plate. "Not going anywhere, but you might want to think about hiding the trowels. I dug a fucking huge hole last night in my dreams, and I have no idea why."

"Gold," Tyler announced. "You were looking for the gold, probably."

"I thought you were joking about finding gold."

Tyler dished up bacon and the beans from the small saucepan, which Martin took with a grateful smile.

"I never joke about gold. In that stream it's very likely there will be specks of gold, but you're more likely to find sapphires. When I've checked today's data, you want to help me look for some?"

"Here?"

"Yep, you'll see."

They ate breakfast in companionable silence, as if there hadn't been this whole messy night just gone, and then went their separate ways. Martin to make coffee, and Tyler to check the data coming from the seismometer. It wouldn't be ready to attach to the wider network until he'd run all the right tests, and he was peering at banks of numbers when Martin thrust coffee under his nose.

Tyler exchanged the iPad for the coffee. "Have a look."

Martin took the other chair and scrolled through the data, his interest turning into a frown, which then became a look of confusion. "It's not stable, is it? Do we need to dig it up?"

"Why?" Tyler prompted with interest.

"Your readings are all over the place. You have spikes here that are well outside the expected range."

"See, that would be a seismic event right there." Tyler pointed at one of the spikes that had occurred late yesterday evening. "The ground is constantly moving, thousands of tiny little tremors, that happen way underground, that up here you never feel. They won't rock buildings or destroy towns, but they're there, all the time."

Martin glanced up at him and then down at the screen, and Tyler expected him to say Tyler was talking crap, but he was nodding.

"That would explain the variance," Martin muttered and stabbed at the screen before pinching it to zoom in.

"It's quiet right now, but there are smaller valleys and peaks there."

"Background noise." Tyler loved his subject, and Martin actually seemed interested right now. "That is seismic noise, a persistent vibration of the ground, from all kinds of sources. We don't need that data, but it forms part of the baseline for this station. What we are looking for are clusters of movement, what we call swarms, and linked up to the entire network, it might give us warnings that a larger quake is on the horizon."

Martin handed the iPad back and then sat back in his chair, nursing his coffee, staying quiet as Tyler finished his reports and then submitted them. Together they moved Martin's tent away from the hole he'd dug in his nightmares, and then filled it with loose mud, packing it down.

"Now I need your help." He led Martin to the Jeep and pulled out two five-gallon buckets nestled inside each other and full of pieces of wood and what looked like giant sieves propped up between them. Together they hauled everything up to near the drop stone, and Martin sat and watched as Tyler constructed a frame from pieces of wood with predrilled holes, taking everything closer to the water.

"Ready to look for treasure?"

Martin glanced from the frame to water. "Yep."

He smiled, and Tyler desperately wanted to kiss that smile. He cradled Martin's face gently and smoothed curls with his thumbs.

"Can I kiss you, Martin?"

In response, Martin leaned in and met Tyler halfway, and the kiss was sweet until it turned hot. They kissed enough so that they both ran out of breath, but it was Martin who pulled back.

"Stop trying to distract me from the treasure," he teased.

And all Tyler could think was that he'd just had the treasure in his hands.

He just hoped it wasn't fool's gold and that he would get to see Martin after they were done here.

Chapter Fourteen

Martin had watched the construction with interest and felt comfortable sitting on the drop stone while Tyler worked. He'd woken up this morning feeling as if there had been a seismic shift in him after the nightmare and the subsequent hug in the dark. Yes, Tyler hadn't been in bed when Martin woke, but contrary to what he'd feared, everything seemed easy between them.

Some of the things he'd exposed last night, some of the pain he'd let out? That had been cathartic, a liberating experience to unload some of his inner worries onto someone who'd just held his hand and let him talk. The only other person he'd talked to was his counselor, and she'd been of the opinion that he was stronger than he thought he was.

Then that kiss just now, the way Tyler had cradled his face, the absolute thoroughness with which he'd tasted Martin had Martin feeling more than a little dazed.

"You want to help me?" Tyler asked, standing right in front of him, his body blocking the sunlight.

"To find gold?"

Tyler grinned. "As I said, probably no more than a few flakes of gold, but we'll probably find…" He counted each gem on a finger, "Jasper, garnet, several varieties of quartz, rhodonite, serpentine, staurolite, topaz, tourmaline, and wonderstone. And of course sapphires if we're lucky." He held up his hand and waggled his fingers. "Come on, it's fun, and you never know, you might turn into someone who won't be able to pass by a rock without picking it up for a closer look. You could be a closet rock hound."

"I might have enough personal baggage to open a suitcase store, but I'm not a closet anything," Martin said as he stood and stretched tall. He saw Tyler's gaze rest on him and rake him from head to toe, and suddenly he felt warmer than the pale May sun warranted. "What?" he asked and checked his shirt to see if he'd spilled something because Tyler's gaze was so damn focused. Then he was up in Martin's space and pulling him in for another kiss. It wasn't deep or driven by sex. It was simple and soft, and when he pulled back, he was smiling.

"I could kiss you all morning," he said.

And there it was. In those simple words, he was acknowledging the shift between them, and from the smile, he seemed happy enough.

"You're trying to change the subject away from the gold, aren't you?" Martin replied, then tangled his hand in Tyler's shirt to steal his own soft kiss. "Now show me how I strike gold."

"Not gold—"

"I know, you said jasper, garnet, several varieties of quartz, rhodonite, serpentine, staurolite, topaz, tourmaline, and wonderstone. And of course sapphires if we're lucky," Martin repeated Tyler's words back to him verbatim, and Tyler's eyes widened. "Told you, eidetic memory."

"You should use that, you know," Tyler began earnestly. "Use your memory to learn all kinds of things." *Find a purpose. Live a different life.*

Martin heard the unspoken words but kept things light. "Why would I do that when I already have a degree in mathematics focusing on fractal geometry?" That was his drop-the-mic moment, and he walked away then, heading for the stream, Tyler falling into step with him.

"You're a dark horse," he commented.

"I like numbers. They don't change."

Not like people. Not like my life.

He got the sense that Tyler wanted to ask more, but he didn't want the settled vibe as they searched for gems to be broken. "Banana, no questions," he murmured.

Tyler chuckled. "Got it."

They stopped by the table contraption, a selection of rectangle sieves, and a bag of what appeared to be river bed gravel. Certainly he couldn't see any bright blue sapphires peeking out of the bag.

"So Montana is called the Treasure State for a reason," Tyler began, then dipped his head. "Shit, sorry."

"What for?"

"For starting the explanation as if I was giving a lecture."

"No, go for it. I want to know everything." Martin

tapped his head. "I have space in here if I push out some of the memories of the way you burn bacon."

That earned him a quick kiss, but Tyler moved away before it deepened, which was keeping Martin in a steady state of need.

Tyler cleared his throat. "First off, the bacon was crispy, not burned, and it was your fault for looking so sexy when you woke up."

"Burned," Martin poked.

"I'm ignoring you now. Lots of miners back in the nineteenth century would keep gold and throw away all the pretty stones they thought were worthless. The frosted and etched surfaces of many rough sapphires indicate that they are xenocrysts brought by magma carriers during volcanic eruptions." He dipped his head again, and damn it, but the man was blushing. "Well, I find it interesting."

"I do as well."

Tyler brightened, becoming nerdy-geologist in an instant. "They come in all kinds of colors, not just the blue that you think of when you think sapphires. They were in several gravel bars along the river and everyone called them Fancy Montana sapphires because they were fancy colors."

"I get that."

"So we might find some, and the most common color is a pale blue-green. The rarest color is a true red, which is technically a ruby, but these are almost never found."

"Okay, so what's first?"

"This is a bag of alluvial deposits, which is loose soil or sediment that has been eroded, reshaped by water in some form, and redeposited in a non-marine setting. At least that is the dictionary definition. It has fine particles of silt and clay and larger particles of sand and gravel. We need to sort this into sizes. We're not worried about the huge pieces of gravel. We're looking for the tiny ones. We'll collect quarter- and eighth-inch ones into separate buckets."

As he spoke, he tipped some of the contents of the sack into the first sieve, and Martin was less watching him work and more cataloging each animated micro-expression, the love for the stones he was looking at, the impatience to see if he could find the tiny gems. Martin couldn't recall the last time he'd seen such passion. Then it hit him. He'd seen it recently. Nate and his horses, or Justin and his family, or Sam for his food. It was everywhere at Crooked Tree, and Martin needed to soak some of that up.

Maybe I should stay around for a few days longer?

"So, at the moment these eighth-inch stones look like nothing, but then we need to wash them, and normally I'd set up a process to do that, but for now, we can just use the stream here."

After carefully running water over them, he tipped the sieve upside down in a smooth movement onto a flat board that he had rested on the wooden frame he'd used for sieving.

"Now it looks like a pile of washed eighth-inch stones," Martin teased, suddenly nervous that he'd actually forgotten how to do teasing altogether.

Tyler wrinkled his nose, then stared at the stones. "You're not wrong, but..." He poked around in the stones with a tiny metal tool with retractable claws on the end. "Open your hand," he instructed, and Martin did as he was told. "This I think is serpentine." He retracted the claw, and a tiny stone fell onto Martin's hand. It was a dull green and so small that Martin had to peer really close. But it was there, on his palm, a gem, probably millions of years old, and found by Tyler in a sack of gravel.

"Oh my god," Martin said with reverence. He couldn't quite believe what he was holding.

"And this…" Tyler placed another tiny stone next to the first. It didn't look like a gem, and Martin smiled. "Yep, thought so. That's wonderstone. It's a kind of jasper, and it's supposed to eliminate your worries and tensions."

That made Martin glance up, right into Tyler's hazel eyes. "You believe in all of that?"

Tyler seemed confused for a moment; then his expression cleared. "You mean the healing power of stones?" He shrugged. "I know that these tiny things come from deep in the earth, and better people than me think they are imbued with powers."

"I wonder if there is a stone that can help store some memories for me," Martin said and only realized he'd spoken out loud when Tyler gripped his shoulder.

"Some people say that black jade defends against violence and fear in times of crisis or turmoil. But you know what I think?"

"What?"

"You don't need a stone to defend yourself. You're a strong man, brave to have survived what you went through, and one day you might even see it."

He punctuated the assertion with a kiss, and this time it was just as needy and deep as every other one they'd shared. So much so that Martin closed his hand into a fist around the gems so he didn't lose them. He was so hard, Tyler was hard, they were in the middle of nowhere, the sun stronger on their backs, and they could fall to the ground right here and take what they were doing all the way. But again, it was Tyler who stopped what they were doing.

"Come on," he said and poked Martin in the side. "Start at one corner and work your way in, put unwanted stones back in the bucket."

"What if I throw away a ruby?"

"Then one day, another two guys will be sitting right here and will pick up gravel and find it, instead."

Martin sighed. "I don't like those two guys already."

Tyler laughed and bent over his small corner, and they spent a couple of hours looking through the stones. Ten or so minutes in, Martin went back for the chairs and coffee and the last remaining cookies, and they sat opposite each other working, sharing their finds, Martin asking all kinds of questions. By the time they'd finished, they had a clear bag containing five separate gems, miniature glimpses into Montana's past where volcanoes, earthquakes, and ice had shaped the landscape.

Martin didn't think he'd talked as much in years, but Tyler made everything so simple. They didn't discuss the big things. They talked geology, rubies, walking, photography, anything that didn't touch on the mess he'd revealed last night.

"I wonder how much all of this is worth?" Martin said as he held up the bag to the light.

"Hardly a thing, and we can't keep it anyway. You need to give it to the guys at Crooked Tree."

Temper flared inside Martin. "Are you saying I'd keep it?" he defended immediately.

"No, I didn't mean that at all."

Martin shut his eyes. "Shit, sorry." His temper was typically pushed down so far it barely ever reached the surface, but he'd been judged for things so many times he'd taken everything the wrong way. That had been twice now he'd lost control with Tyler. Two times too many that he'd let the bad side of himself out.

"Why are you sorry?"

"For snapping at you. I know you weren't… that you didn't—"

Tyler stopped him from talking with another one of those incendiary kisses, and when he pulled back, Martin chased for more.

"Come on, let's clean this up."

"We're stopping?" Disappointment coursed through Martin. He'd enjoyed working with Tyler, the stones, the sun shining on them, and he didn't want it to end. How had something so simple been the best thing he'd done in his entire life?

"Only done for today. I have to do some more work, and we can pick this up in the morning. Maybe you could come and help me find some alluvial stones, work it through from the start?"

"Okay."

"Your turn for dinner," Tyler said.

"I'll try not to burn the bacon."

"We've run out of bacon." Tyler shrugged.

They cleared up as they bantered, and headed back to the camp, splitting off, Tyler to do his checks, Martin to start dinner, which left Martin with way too much time to think about what the hell he was doing with Tyler. Everything started simple enough; he relaxed in the chair, head tipped back, watching fluffy spring clouds amble across the cornflower-blue sky, breathing in the fresh Montana air.

Tyler could be good for him, seemed like he was the kind of man who might listen to what Martin had to say and not judge him for it. The way he'd spooned him last night, holding his hand, giving him something to cling to left Martin feeling warm and relaxed. In the camp, there was no room for his past, no room for the memories he hadn't shared with Tyler.

He sat up. What would Tyler do if he knew who his father was? Or worse, what his father had done? What if when they went back to Crooked Tree, Justin turned to Tyler and explained about the murders and the way the group had held Justin and Adam prisoner and the terror attacks they'd spoken of? What about the stadiums they'd wanted to bomb and the people they'd wanted to kill.

What about the chaos they had designed to bring the US to its knees.

How could anyone in their right minds want to be anywhere near someone with that kind of blood in their veins?

His dad's ghost had reared up in him last night. The horrific murderous intent that his dad had warned him was inside Martin, and maybe one day he'd lose control of it and hurt someone. He'd always said, with great pride, that his son might seem like a quiet one but that he actually was a grenade waiting for the pin to be pulled. Of course, being gay was beaten out of him. That was just a weakness.

Martin wished he knew more about his mom and what she'd been like. It wasn't as if he'd be able to connect to her now with her dead and buried. The only real reference he could ever have was his sister, but he'd promised to stay away from her, and he never broke a promise.

He'd often wondered if Alice had the same darkness inside her, but always decided she couldn't be like him because Mom hadn't left her; she'd left Martin.

Mom left because she thought that one day I'd be like him.

"Fuck, where is all this coming from?" he muttered to the trees. He was spiraling and losing his fricking mind. The only thing that had changed was Tyler, and it must be Tyler and his compassion, digging under his skin, burrowing past his defenses, and making him weak. Leaving him open to all these dark thoughts. He needed to rewind things, go back to the creek, look for shiny gems, and forget all the crap in his brain. But his dad's words were there.

You can be anything, son. Burn women and children, slit their husband's throats as they watch. Hell, you can be the very worst kind of killer and change the whole fucking world. I know you can be that, but don't ever be weak. Don't be gay.

Martin closed his eyes tight. The words he could never forget shouted at him when he'd missed the target at shooting practice. He hadn't recalled those words in the longest time, and the nightmare had clearly unleashed something inside him, a deluge of thoughts he hadn't even considered when they'd been searching for gems. His dad had been right about only one thing, though.

Martin wasn't a killer, but he would never allow himself to be weak.

That way he'd stay safe.

All he needed to do was back away from Tyler.

I don't want to.

Chapter Fifteen

SOMETHING HAD CHANGED SINCE FINDING THE gemstones Tyler thought as he headed back to camp for dinner. First off, Martin was nowhere to be found, and second, there was no sign of dinner preparation. It was as if Martin had disappeared from the map, and that was unsettling.

"Martin?"

"Over here," a faint voice called, and relieved, Tyler went in that direction and found Martin lying on the ground under a break in the canopy of trees.

"Is everything okay?"

Martin rolled to his feet, brushing dirt off his jeans. "Why wouldn't I be okay?"

"I couldn't see you, and dinner isn't—"

"I don't think I signed up to be the fucking cook," Martin snapped and then strode past him toward camp.

"I never said you did, but you said you were going to…"

Martin wasn't listening. He went into his tent and

zipped himself in, and there was clearly something very wrong.

Tyler went straight to the tent and knocked on the upright. "Martin, open up."

Silence.

Seemed as if he just needed his space, so Tyler did what every worried lover did, he sat right outside the tent and waited.

"I'm going to sit here and wait for you to come out. If I can help, then I want to. So you maybe need to come out, Martin, and talk to me."

Nothing.

"I hope you're okay, Martin. I mean, I could unzip this tent now and just find out if you're okay. But I won't." Tyler looked at the sky, just as Martin would do. "You can't see the sky in there," he mused. "You should come out and see the sky with me and tell me what happened in the space of time I wasn't here. No? Okay, well, I'll just sit here and talk."

He fetched his chair and settled more comfortably, with a bottle of water in hand, by the zipped entrance. Then he did what he did best. He talked.

"Way back in 1879, prospectors found small amounts of gold in this place called Yogo Creek. It was just a small stream, and they didn't find a lot of gold. But in their sieving were all of these bright blue pebbles, but even though they were pretty, they weren't gold. So the prospectors threw them back into the water. All those blue sapphires, tossed away as if they weren't worth a thing. Except one day, fifteen years or so later, there was this one guy who sent a small amount of these blue pebbles to a gold assayer, who forwarded them on to Tiffany's in New York—"

"Banana," Martin snapped loudly, angrily.

"I can't hear you," Tyler lied. "Anyway, this other guy, George Kunz, he was the chief gemologist at Tiffany's, and he realized what they had, and said they were the finest precious gemstones ever found in the United States. Imagine that. All those years of these men looking for riches, and the earth had offered up the largest deposit of sapphires in the western hemisphere, and they just threw them away. Their world could have been a very different place."

Martin exited his tent with a scowl on his face. "Do you ever shut up?"

Tyler wasted no time, was up out of his seat and between Martin and the tent in an instant. "Talk to me," he demanded. For a while Martin stared at him stubbornly, and then inch by inch, that mulishness dissipated, and vulnerability took its place. He softened his voice. "Tell me what happened, Martin."

"I wouldn't know where to start."

"Did I say something, or do—?"

"Everything's not always about you," Martin interrupted and then visibly slumped. "Fuck."

Tyler was at a loss for what to say. He felt as if he knew Martin, and at the same time, how could he really know him at all. To have lived through abuse and then have casual sex on the side of a mountain must be messing with his mind. He was attracted to Martin, they'd been good together, but he could also just be friends if that was what Martin wanted.

Martin pressed a hand to his chest. "I never meant to stay at Crooked Tree. I just wanted to ask Justin a question, but he won't give me an answer. I should keep running, but what if the very thing I'm trying to get away from is actually inside me all along?"

Tyler waited for Martin to explain more, but that short impassioned snippet of his thought process appeared to be all he was offering.

Martin stepped closer, stared right at Tyler, and then kissed him. Gripped his arms and kissed him hard, demanding entrance, teeth clashing, and his hold tightening. Tyler enjoyed the kiss at first. Martin was hot, turned him on, and the kiss was spectacular until it was less about kissing and more about Martin shoving him back, pushing him to the ground, and kissing him harder. There was no softness in the kiss. It was nothing like they'd had before, and then Tyler tasted the tears. In a smooth move, he levered Martin off him until they lay side by side, Martin panting as if he'd run a race, and Tyler feeling as if they'd somehow moved off course.

"I'm not perfect," Martin said, his voice was thick with tears.

"No one is."

"You don't know everything."

"Maybe I don't need to." He turned his head to glance at Martin, who had tears trickling from his eyes. He rolled onto his side and traced Martin's face with a finger. "I don't know what we have, but I know we can kiss way better than just now." He leaned in, careful not to put any of his weight on Martin, giving him plenty of room to get away, and then he pushed his free hand into Martin's curls. "I want to kiss you."

That was all the warning he was giving. He pressed a gentle kiss to Martin's soft lips before backing away. Then, after a short pause, another. Then another. And finally Martin parted his lips and joined in. The sun was warm on his back, the ground hard, the touch of Martin's lips hot, and he didn't argue when Tyler slid a hand up under his top and rubbed his fingers over Martin's nipples before circling them down to his belly.

Somehow Tyler moved enough so Martin sprawled on top of him, and the kisses became more, clothes were removed, slowly, and finally bare-chested, they lay together, joined at the lips, and with Tyler's hand returning to Martin's hair. Martin kissed his way down to Tyler's throat, resting there a minute, his ear over Tyler's heart, and then he focused on kissing a trail from nipple to nipple, worrying at them, sucking and pulling until Tyler thought he was going to lose it from that alone. He pushed his hips up, but Martin moved, unbuckled Tyler's jeans, pulled them down a little, along with his boxers, and then he looked up at Tyler.

"Is this okay?"

"If the question is you sucking me off, then…" He had no more words, because Martin closed his lips around the head of Tyler's cock and sucked him deep, then licked his way along the length of him. He captured the head again in his mouth. Then his lips slid a few inches down the shaft, his mouth stretched wide around the thickness of the cock. When he repeated the motion, his head moving, his eyes closed, it took everything for Tyler not to come.

With Martin's hands firm on Tyler's hip bones, he was immobile, but that didn't stop him from resting his fingers on Martin's head, smoothing the curls, and losing himself to sensation.

"So close," he warned, but Martin didn't pull off. If anything, he intensified his sucking then released the suction on Tyler's cock, moved up to kiss him, tugging at a nipple, pinching it, and wrapping his other hand around Tyler's cock, and *fuck*, that was game over, and he was done. He arched up, pushed against Martin, shouted his release, the noise lost in the kiss, and when he slumped back to earth, Martin sat back on his heels and opened his buckle, reaching in enough to get his hands on his cock. His eyes were wide open, and he stared down at Tyler, unflinching, as he got himself off. Tyler tried to reach for him, but Martin swatted his hand away.

"Too close," he warned, leaning down, capturing a kiss, and then stiffening as he reached orgasm. He groaned into the kiss, then fell boneless half on top of Tyler, who pulled him close and held him tight.

"We're so good together. I've never had... not before this..." Martin didn't know what he was trying to say. A thank you maybe or a hell yes or possibly he was begging for more. "That was hot. You and me, we fit. When we get back, I want to see you again. Can we do that? I'm not always near here, but fuck, you need to stay around here or come with me, and we need to do this a lot. Like *a lot*."

Martin closed his eyes then and rolled off, grabbing a T-shirt and wiping at the mess between them.

"I don't know what I'm doing or what I even *can* do."

"Well, whatever it is, maybe one day we could make love in a bed. I'm not getting any younger."

Martin sent him a glance that was almost shy.

They redressed, minus the wet T-shirt, and then Tyler extended his hand.

"I have something to show you."

There was a definite hesitation, but Martin finally

took his hand, and Tyler led him to the supplies tent. He released his hold and looked for one container in particular.

"I take this everywhere with me," he began and opened the small box to show Martin the array of gems and stones inside. "This is my collection." They weren't in any kind of order. This wasn't for display; this was all about memories. He rummaged through them and found what he was looking for. "This is Angel Aura Quartz, and it was a present from my dad the day I came out to him and my mom." He turned it over in his fingers and then held it up to the light. "Can you see that?"

"It's a prism."

"Yeah. Dad went on about its otherworldly properties, but he was big on *Lord of the Rings*, and he said that it looked as if it was from an ethereal realm. I just let him talk because he and mom had listened to my impassioned coming out speech and told me everything was okay. I think he didn't know what to say next, so he started talking about crystals. I inherited that from him, I think."

"Seems that way," Martin murmured.

Tyler smiled. "And Mom, because you should hear her talk about sixteenth-century poetry. I owed my dad to listen to him rambling on about this particular metal-coated crystal and how people liked to think it held magic, but all I could think was that it was perfect, even though it has cracks and hollows. He let me keep it. I was fourteen, and it comes with me everywhere. And now, you can have it." He held it out to Martin.

"What? Why?"

"Because it's been my good luck charm, and I don't need it anymore, and you do right now."

"I'm can't take what your dad—"

"I'm not arguing, Martin. Take it." He jiggled his hand a little, and finally Martin picked up the beautiful crystal and held it up to the sunshine, and he smiled. Not a wide grin of happiness but a slight smile of appreciation. "Keep it with you, and it will bring you luck."

"Surely you don't really believe that?"

Tyler couldn't lie. "No, but my dad did, and I think that him feeling that way means it's special. So now it's for you, wherever it takes you."

"If only something this simple could make a real difference to the mess in my head."

They were interrupted by a loud beep from Tyler's iPad. "More results are in," he said, kind of pissed the results happened to arrive right at this freaking minute. "Put the stone in your pocket. Keep it safe."

"I will," Martin peered at the stone, and his expression remained skeptical.

Tyler trusted that his dad's belief in him was always there. He hadn't needed a stone to know that, but maybe Martin needed a crystal that held rainbows.

Something small might be just enough.

Chapter Sixteen

THE LAST FEW DAYS ON THE SITE WERE ABOUT TESTS, more tests, and in between there was kissing and frotting and some talking. Not a lot of talking from him; it was mostly Tyler. Martin loved how enthusiastic he was about things, and when he told his stories, his words had a lyrical quality. Some of what he said was technical, some of it about mining history. On two occasions, they even talked for the longest time about the kind of movies they liked.

When it came to the final day, and there was packing up to be done, Tyler vanished. At first, Martin put it down to Tyler avoiding the heavy lifting, but they were taking back less than half of what they'd come with. After half an hour, Martin went looking and found him standing by the creek where it tumbled out of the rocks in the mountain.

"Looking for gold still?" he queried, and Tyler turned to face him, a smile on his face.

"No, just thinking about things."

Tyler didn't owe him an explanation about his

thoughts, but Martin asked anyway, "What kind of things?"

"Are you staying at Crooked Tree after all of this? Did what we have here change how you feel?"

"About Crooked Tree? No. There's no place for me here; I need to move on."

"Where will you go?"

It was on the tip of Martin's tongue to say south, but that wasn't true anymore, so he offered the only thing he could, "I don't know."

"I have an apartment, in Billings. It's home for when I'm there. You could come and live with me."

He sounded as if he'd given this thought and seemed hopeful that Martin would say yes. Staying in a city? Living with someone? How could he do that when so many unspoken things stood between them? Tyler didn't know about his dad, not the real story.

"That wouldn't work," Martin said, forcing his hands into his jean pockets, the fingers of his right hand closing around the rainbow crystal.

"It could if you gave it a try. Then you could find a job in the city, and we could see how this thing between us goes."

"There is no 'thing,' Tyler. This was a short time of fun, and I loved it, and you saw more of me than any man ever has done, but when we get back, it has to be finished."

Tyler shook his head. "I won't accept that."

Martin desperately wanted to back down, to say that everything could continue, that he would move in and that one day they'd share that they loved each other and live happily ever after. But it wasn't true.

"What you accept is your choice, but after we get

back, I have one more thing to do and then I'm leaving."

"Can I say anything to make you change your mind?" Tyler sounded lost. "What if I told you I think I could fall in love with you, that maybe I'm already halfway there?"

Hope flared in his chest, but he ruthlessly pushed it down. "You don't know me, so you can't feel those things."

"I know enough. I know that when we kiss it's perfect and when we make love it's the best feeling I've ever felt."

Martin needed to get him to stop, by any means possible. "We didn't make love. We fucked, we had sex, we were in an isolated camp, and it was convenient." The words came out harsher than he'd expected them to, and he waited for Tyler to punch him.

Tyler let out a hollow laugh. "Fuck you, Martin."

"Look, let's get the Jeep packed. We want to be back at the ranch before dark." Martin began to head down the hill and ignored Tyler calling his name. What he couldn't ignore was Tyler grabbing his arm and pulling him to a stop.

"I won't let you leave just like that. We can talk. We can fix all the things that are making you run scared. Martin, please listen to me—"

"Banana. Okay? Stop," Martin said and yanked his arm free.

Tyler didn't tug him back again or talk further. In fact, the journey back to Crooked Tree was mostly done in silence. Tyler drove, Martin kept an eye on the navigation, and just as dusk painted the sky with mauves and reds, they pulled up outside cabin six, and Tyler killed the engine.

"Help me get everything inside?" he asked, and Martin nodded.

Together they emptied the contents of the Jeep into a spare room in the cabin, and as Tyler finished his short call to Jay to tell him they were back safely, Martin left. What was the point in stretching this out? He had to pull the Band-Aid off in one go, and that way no one would get hurt.

"Martin, wait."

Against his better judgment, Martin turned to look at him. "What?"

"One night. Okay? Let's just finish this right, take a bath, showers, give ourselves some memories?"

"That's not a wise idea."

"It is. It's everything I want right now, and then afterward, you can go, and I won't stop you. I won't go after you. I won't tell you how I'm starting to feel. I'll accept you'll go."

Anger poked at him, and he stalked back toward Tyler. "Why won't you leave this alone?" He was torn between wanting to touch Tyler and knowing he should run as if the hounds of hell were nipping at his heels.

In the end, it was no choice at all because Tyler unbuttoned his shirt, yanked off his T-shirt, and unbuckled his jeans, leaving a trail of clothes from the front door. Martin heard the shower, and the temptation to kiss Tyler just a few more times, to give himself some extra memories gave him pause. What if they had just one more night? Would it even matter? It was just one more fuck, and then Martin could move on. He shut the front door behind him and headed for the bathroom and the sound of running water.

He hesitated by the shower, even though Tyler opened the wide door and was already soaping his gorgeous body. Martin wanted to be in there, and he'd already committed himself just by coming inside the cabin, let alone taking his clothes off by the shower.

Was it too much to ask for just one last evening of perfect? Tyler wasn't forcing him to stay. He'd explicitly said this was goodbye, so what would it hurt to step inside?

"Are you coming in?" Tyler asked, smoothing his hands over his chest, a trail of soap bubbles catching on his hips, then sliding down over his erection and his thighs, joining the water swirling around the plug. Martin watched every single bubble disappear, then looked up and met Tyler's heated gaze.

"I want to," Martin admitted.

"Once more," Tyler encouraged, and the simple words meant everything to Martin. There was a time limit on what they had, and it fit with his expectations; he felt calm. He stepped in, and Tyler encouraged him under the water, soaping him from head to toe, going to his knees and paying special attention to Martin's cock. He was close right there in the shower, but it appeared that Tyler had different ideas. He toweled them off, then took Martin's hand, tugging him to the bedroom and holding up condoms.

"Will you... can we... make love to me?"

Martin linked the words together, but it was only when Tyler went to all fours on the bed, that everything made perfect sense. But he didn't want that position; he wanted to see Tyler's face.

"On your back, please," he pleaded.

Tyler turned immediately, his cock hard, and a knowing expression on his face. "Come on then," he goaded, and Martin wasn't going to be told twice.

Everything was slow, and hot, and Buried deep in Tyler, kissing him, watching his face as he was coming, and it was all too much, with Martin's orgasm slamming into him.

"I want you to think about coming with me to Billings," Tyler said, his voice muffled from where his face was buried in Martin's neck. Martin had cleaned up, disposed of the condom, and spent an extra two minutes staring at himself in the bathroom mirror wondering how he'd gotten so lucky.

"It would kill me to have to live in a city," Martin said. "I need the sky. I want isolation."

"Like Crooked Tree can be for you."

"I guess." He hadn't thought the place he was describing could be Crooked Tree. There wasn't a chance he'd be able to stay there, and nor did he want to. He was leaving tomorrow before his presence messed up things for Justin and Adam.

Just the thought of the two men had him shutting his eyes tight and rolling onto his side, burying his face in the pillow, facing away from Tyler. All Tyler did in response was spoon him from behind, his strong grip holding Martin still.

"I know I said tonight was the final time, but we have something, Martin. I could buy somewhere else, a place in the middle of nowhere that you can come home to when it gets too much. I have a trust fund. I know I don't look like I do, but my dad wrote books. Look, what I'm saying is that money isn't an issue."

Martin stiffened in Tyler's hold and attempted to squirm away, finally breaking free and sitting up on the side of the bed.

"Why won't you take no for an answer?" he asked and heard Tyler sigh.

"Because I've never met anyone like you, because we could be good together, because I could make you happy if you let me."

"You don't know me."

"I know about Xander. I know you have nightmares. I know something is eating away at you, scaring you, and making you wary. But I also know that you have the most beautiful smile, and that you laugh with your whole body, and that you put yourself in the way to stop me from getting hurt when I fell. You're a good man, Martin, and you need to let me be able to tell you that."

Years of insecurity and guilt washed over him. "No, I'm not."

"Not what?"

"A good man." He suddenly felt miserable, alone, and overwhelmed.

"I couldn't fall in love with anyone who wasn't a good man, Martin."

Martin rounded on him. "I helped to lock away two boys. I watched my dad and Xander pour chemicals on them. I watched when they left the boys to die. My dad and his *friends* were the very worst kind of human, and I have that same blood in me. So no, I'm not a good man, and you don't know me at all."

"Martin?" Tyler attempted to reach him, but Martin twisted out of the way and dressed as quickly as he could. All the time, Tyler followed him, trying to touch him. He wouldn't leave Martin alone, and his expression was a mix of horror and sadness. "Talk to me, Martin. Explain what you mean."

"I was part of it," he spat, "and I thought I didn't have a choice, but at any moment I could have told someone what I knew. Anyone. And I didn't." He opened the front door, Tyler hovering behind him but not touching him now. "Try Googling David Crane and see you don't know his son at all."

He left then, stalked up to the cabin where his stuff was, and in a few minutes he was packed and heading off Crooked Tree. He made it as far as the bridge and stopped for a moment, looking at the sky and recalling the day he'd arrived. All he'd wanted to do was see Justin, tell him that he wasn't brave but that somehow he'd found peace of sorts, and everything had gone to shit. He owed it to Justin to explain what he was doing. Somehow he knew that, and he headed up to Branches and the door on the side that led up to Justin's place.

He knocked, and the door opened after a few moments, Justin crossing his arms over his chest and staring out at Martin.

Sucking up every ounce of bravery, he copied Justin's stance.

"I asked why you let me live, but you won't tell me, and I'm fucking done with it all."

He turned to leave and got almost six paces away when Justin called after him.

"You're a coward, Jamie Crane."

Martin winced at the use of his name, still not able to hear anyone call him that, and he stopped walking.

"Hell yes, I'm a coward," he agreed, then turned to face Justin, who'd stepped out of his door and was only a couple of feet behind him. "You don't need to tell me that."

"But, you're also the bravest person I have ever met."

Martin dumped his bag to the ground and moved right up into Justin's face. "Fuck you for saying that shit," he shouted.

"You left the doors open," Justin repeated what he'd said that first night.

"So the fuck what? I left two doors open, so yeah, I'm a freaking superhero."

"We saw what he did to you. We saw him beat you and demean you. We saw how scared you were. You were a terrified child the same as we were."

Martin shoved him so hard that Justin stumbled back, but he found his balance and stood his ground, holding out a hand to grab Martin's jacket. Martin panicked, ripped himself away, and ended up on his ass in the mud. Hell, he couldn't even do leaving right.

"You faced me. Do you know how brave that is, Jamie? You came right up to me, and you were vulnerable, and yet you faced me. But if you leave now, you will never face up to Adam."

"He doesn't need to see me."

"Yeah, he does. He's home on Friday, three more days. You stay, see Adam, and then maybe you'll get over this shit about you being like your dad."

The punch was instinctive. He clenched his fist and punched Justin in the face, square on the mouth, the temper in him so high.

"I'm just like him!"

Justin gripped his hands, stopped him from moving, and the panic was a flutter of pain in his chest. "I'll let you have that one. But right now, I have a question for you: the devices that the group was going to plant in the Cowboys stadium, how many of them did you help build?"

"What?" He tried to shake free, but Justin wasn't letting him go.

"How many devices meant to kill hundreds did you help to build?"

"None of them. I didn't know…" He yanked again.

Justin tightened his hold, so much that it began to hurt. "What did you do? Did you research the best place to cause the most deaths? Did you source materials? Did you make deals with drug dealers to finance the terror?"

"No." This time he managed to get free. "I didn't even know… I was in my own fucking world, grieving Levi, and I should have known." He rubbed at his wrists, and tears choked his voice.

"How could you have known?" Justin's voice was even, and Martin watched the blood oozing from his cut lip. He'd done that, hurt another person and made them bleed.

"I was there, for fuck's sake."

"Why don't you like enclosed spaces?"

That question was so left field that Martin didn't know how to answer.

"I don't know," he said, frantically pushing down his fear.

"Yes, you do," Justin murmured. "Tell me why you don't like being stuck somewhere with no way out."

"I don't fucking know!" Martin shouted. He didn't care who heard him, but Justin pulled him into his place and shut the door. Then he crowded Martin up against it, overwhelming him, his face so close that Martin couldn't breathe. Martin shoved, but Justin didn't move, and suddenly Martin cracked, pushing hard, anything to get out of the space.

"Tell me," Justin insisted.

"They locked me away!" Martin cried, tears rolling down his face, "Dad had this shack. It was dark, no windows, and they locked me in there, Xander was the only one who visited." The tears were violent now, pulled from deep inside him, and he shook, sliding down the wall to sit on the floor, drawing up his knees and burying his face in his hands. He couldn't breathe, but at least Justin moved away from him.

"You didn't have anything to do with what happened to Adam and me, not really. You took a beating to keep Adam safe. You pulled Xander off him, I know. I remember it all. Then when you could have been caught, you deliberately left the doors unlocked, and you looked at me. Do you remember that?"

"No, there's nothing. That last day, I don't remember much at all."

"You told me to get Adam and run. You were terrified, lost, but you still helped us. You still told us to *run*."

Shards of that day spun in his head, but he'd been petrified, and he couldn't recall everything in detail, only that he had to get away.

"I lost everything." He'd lost his mom, his childhood, his innocence. "But what kind of man was I that I *let* these things happen?"

Justin let out a humorless chuckle. "You were fourteen. You weren't a man, Jamie, any more than Adam and I were. It's what you make of things now. That is what makes you a man. I know you tried to stop the fire at the café, that you went in there with an extinguisher, and you tried to save the place."

"I couldn't save it, the fire was too far gone."

"Adam is back Friday. Stay that long, yeah? Just see him, and you might have one less weight you are determined to carry around with you. Then maybe I'll answer your question."

Sam appeared at the top of the stairs and came down to sit next to Justin.

"Hey," he said.

That was so out of character for Sam, that Martin did a double take.

Sam tapped the wall. "Sorry, thin walls. I heard everything."

Martin closed his eyes briefly. The shame of being heard losing his shit was fire in his veins, his skin hot with it.

Sam hadn't finished though. "I wanted to say thank you, for helping Justin and Adam, for everything you did in that moment that means I get to be in love with Justin now." He curled his hand into Justin's and held tight. "That's destiny, right there."

Was Justin right about all of this? Could Martin actually be a good man?

Can I be loved?

"Until Adam," he murmured and then used the wall to stand up, shaky and light-headed. He scrubbed at his eyes, and when he opened them, Justin was holding out a hand to shake. He acted on instinct and shook his hand and then Sam's.

"You have a sister," Justin said as Martin turned to leave.

He paused with his hand on the door. "I don't, not

really. Her stepdad was adamant she didn't need me, said I wasn't fit to know her. He's right."

Justin didn't reply, but let out a heartfelt sigh.

"I have something for you." Martin pulled out the bag of tiny gems and passed them to Justin. "We found these in the gravel by the creek. Tyler says there are more, and I don't think they are worth anything, but they're pretty."

Justin took the bag and shook the gems. Thank. "Thank you."

When Martin stepped out in the colder May night, with the scent of snow in the air, he pulled his jacket close and headed back to the bridge, standing there for a long time, soaking in the peace of the ranch and the stars in the vast blackness.

He couldn't help wondering what Tyler thought of him now. Had he Googled Martin's dad, had he read the limited news articles that talked of unacted-upon plans? None of them went into detail, but the label—domestic terrorist—would be enough for Tyler to draw a picture in his head. Radicalism, hate, terror, and all of that in Martin's blood.

Half of it. The other half of him was his mom, but she'd left him.

Could he be a better man? Could he be more than the sum of the parts that created him?

He stopped at the bridge again, standing in the shadows and listening to the water crashing against the boulders below, wondering if any of them were drop stones and circling back to thinking about Tyler. He'd dumped all of his self-hatred on Tyler, told him to look up his dad, told him the very worst of the things he took the blame for, and Tyler hadn't done anything to deserve that. He reached the end of the bridge.

If he turned left, he would be taking the long, winding track to the main road, where, if he was lucky, he could find a passing car. He had money owed to him from the work he'd done with Tyler, but that would mean staying here, and he didn't want the money. He didn't want anything more to do with Tyler.

Liar.

If he turned right, and he'd be heading back down to his cabin, and past what was Tyler's place. Turn right and he would be committing to staying until Friday when he could do what he came to do: speak to Adam and lay some ghosts to rest. Maybe get an answer from Justin.

He headed for his cabin, but as he drew closer, when he should be taking a side path, he stayed on the main one and walked until he was really close to Tyler's. There were lights on, more than when he'd left, and he stopped where he was, staring at the cabin from a distance. There was movement by the front door, and then it was flung open, and Tyler, bundled up, stalked out and began to walk in his direction. He came to an abrupt stop when he spotted Martin, and there were at least six feet between them.

"I thought you'd left," he said and held up his keys. "I was coming to find you. I mean, I don't know where you'd gone, but I figured you couldn't have had much of a head start, and I could catch up and bring you back." He stopped talking all by himself and stepped closer, his expression uncertain. "I didn't Google your dad."

"Why? You should. Then you could see what—"

"I'm not interested in who your dad was, I'm

interested in *you*. I don't believe what you told me. I mean, I believe you were there. I understand you saw this, but I am your friend, and I know that you—"

"You don't know anything," Martin began, but he wasn't angry or disbelieving. He was just sad. "But I can tell you if you want?"

He'd left himself wide open, finally, after all this time, allowing himself to be vulnerable, and the ball was in Tyler's court. Tyler cradled his face and kissed him gently.

"Let's go inside."

Chapter Seventeen

TYLER LISTENED TO THE STORY OF MARTIN'S LIFE AND went from sickened at what had happened to him, to furious that he was taking any blame. They'd started sitting opposite each other on separate sofas but ended up next to each other, holding hands or more as if clinging on for dear life.

"And your mom never came back?" That was the one thing that made no sense at all. How could a mother leave a child?

Martin shrugged, and Tyler wished he could take away the despair in every line of him.

"So now you know." Martin stood, shaking off Taylor's hold. "I owed you that much, so you know, in case…"

"In case of what?"

There was another shrug then, and Tyler didn't want to see a shrug. What he actually wanted was to kiss Martin again and then lie in bed together and just hug. He got the feeling Martin hadn't had a lot of hugs in his life, and Tyler could be the person who dispensed hugs at the drop of a hat.

"Stay and sleep with me. Just sleeping, nothing else, except maybe more talking."

"I'm tired."

Tyler held out a hand, which Martin took. "Let's go to bed."

They undressed, climbed into bed, and Tyler pulled Martin into his arms. He stroked Martin's back in a slow rhythm and waited for him to talk if he wanted to. There was so much that Tyler wanted to say, about how when Martin wasn't with him he felt bereft, and how much he'd loved having Martin with him at the installation. But this was Martin's call, and when his breathing deepened and he fell asleep, all Tyler did was hold him close to reassure him that he never wanted to let go.

Somehow, he slept as well, although it wasn't restful. Every time he opened his eyes, he expected Martin to have left, but Martin slept on, and Tyler was more than just relieved. He was hopeful.

Wanting to make things right for Martin wasn't a bad thing, right? He always knew that one day he'd meet a man he'd connect with, who'd listen to him ramble and know when to stop him. Someone whose kisses would send Tyler flying, and whose touch would be enough to reduce him to a thing of pure need.

Was this love?

He thought it was. His mom and dad had met at sixteen, fallen in love at first sight, and were so in love still. They argued, they made up, they had wildly different interests, but they were connected by the love they had for each other and for their children. What was it like for someone not to have that solid unit backing them up? Tyler's mom would love Martin, tease him for his wavy hair, make him her trademark lasagna, try to guide him to her side in family debates. And knowing Martin, he'd be respectfully unable to say no to her, and that would be it. He'd be pulled into the family in an instant.

"I love you," he tested, the words soft and drifting off in the quiet room. Martin didn't move as Tyler spoke, so he repeated them, "Martin, I love you."

"Hmmm?" Martin asked sleepily, wriggling closer to Tyler and letting out a puff of warm breath as he settled back. "Didjasay somethin'?"

"Go back to sleep," Tyler answered, and with a soft grunt of agreement, Martin went back to sleep. Clearly he felt safe in Tyler's arms.

Tyler had never felt so strong.

THE NEXT TIME he woke it was daylight, and Martin was still asleep. For a while Tyler carded his hand through Martin's hair and hummed the first tune that came to mind. He was at peace this morning, and in this silent time, he was lost in thoughts of what Martin would do when he woke up.

It was seven before Martin rolled off him and stretched, then lay still on the bed before turning his head to look at Tyler.

"Morning," he said, his voice scratchy.

"Morning. How are you feeling?"

Martin grimaced. "I feel like I've gone ten rounds with Mike Tyson," he groaned and pushed himself to sit up. He'd need some time to work through what happened last night and how he'd come back, and the best way Tyler could think of doing that was to go and make breakfast. Before he went, he kissed the top of Martin's head.

"I'll get us breakfast. The shower's all yours."

He'd nearly made it out of the door when Martin's soft tone caught him. "We okay?" he asked, uncertain.

That was an easy question to answer. "Always," he said and punctuated the statement with a wink.

He hadn't realized he'd been waiting for the sound of the shower until he heard it. He hadn't imagined how much he wanted to see Martin with him for breakfast until he sat at the table.

Martin picked up a slice of bacon and held it up. "You even burn it on a normal stove?" he said and smiled. He was tired, exhausted even, but there was a new light in his eyes. A hope. Or at least Tyler thought that was what he was seeing.

"I wanted to give you that authentic camping experience."

They finished the bacon, eggs, and toast, and then it got to the point where they needed to start their day. Tyler had work to do on the reports and was due back in Butte at the university on Thursday, and Martin admitted he didn't know what they wanted him to do, but he was going up to Crooked Tree to find something.

THURSDAY ARRIVED TOO SOON, and Tyler found that having to leave was one of the hardest things he'd ever done.

"I love you," he said as they kissed goodbye. He didn't want to part without saying those words to

Martin. "I'm coming back to Crooked Tree next weekend. Will you be here?"

Martin wouldn't quite meet his eyes.

"I might be," he hedged.

"If you're not here, then I promise I'll try to find you, just so I can keep telling you that I love you."

He wasn't going to fail in finding Martin.

Chapter Eighteen

Martin missed Tyler already, acutely aware that he'd become his touchstone over these last few days. They'd met up every evening and eaten dinner together, spent some time talking about life, and a lot about geology and coffee and anything else that sounded interesting. Staying here was something he owed to Justin, Adam, and himself. But he also needed to do this so he could confront the last of his ghosts.

Today was the day in which Adam was returning, and Martin understood that was why he'd been given tasks that took him away from the main offices. First thing, to clean the River cabins, which he'd finished by ten, and then on to delivering groceries to the families who'd just arrived for their stays. A family of seven was in Tyler's freshly cleaned cabin, and it seemed odd to see new people in the space that had become his safe place and the place where he'd found himself falling in love.

Because he *had* fallen in love. Something monumental had shifted in his life, and it was all due to Justin pushing him and Tyler not letting him go. Tyler didn't know it was Justin and Adam he'd talked about, but releasing the grief and guilt had been cathartic, and one day if Justin and Adam were okay with it, maybe he could tell Tyler everything.

Justin had said it would be easier if Martin was away from the ranch so he could talk to Adam first.

Martin had been working with Jay on the ranch accounts. Not that accounts were his thing, but at least he was good with numbers. Justin asked him to report to Nate at the stables and he wasn't looking forward to it, but he'd try his damnedest to make sure that whatever he did was done quietly and efficiently. His only worry was that Adam was back and somehow he'd be waiting for Martin, and his reaction would probably tear down the fragile confidence he'd started to build. Justin never once said how he thought Adam was going to react to Martin being here. In fact, he was evasive, and Martin didn't want to push.

Today Justin would be explaining to Adam and his partner, Ethan, that the man responsible for hurting Justin and Adam was here.

Later Martin might not have somewhere to stay, and he'd already packed up his meagre belongings in case he needed to run.

It wasn't much. His Martin Graves ID, what little money he had, the cell phone he always kept fully charged, and the rainbow crystal that went with him everywhere. He was ready to go and had made sketchy plans that would never pan out.

The only bright spot among the worry was the text he'd received this morning.

I miss you. Wish you could make it out here. A man can hope. x

Martin wasn't sure they would ever see each other again, but over the past couple of weeks, meeting Tyler, experiencing something normal, had changed him, and he knew it. He wanted to see Tyler again, he just wasn't sure he'd head for the city to do that.

It wasn't Nate waiting for him with the horses, but Justin, his hands pushed into his pockets. There was someone else there, a man with a baseball cap pulled low on his face. At first, Martin didn't recognize him, but as he moved closer, his chest tightened, and his steps faltered. He hadn't changed much from when he was fifteen. This had to be Adam.

Adam. Fuck.

Justin turned to the man and said something low enough that Martin couldn't hope to hear him. Then he stalked toward Martin and brushed his shoulder as he passed.

"Please don't fuck this up," he muttered. "Or I will find you, and I will throw you off Ember Bluff." The way he said it made Martin feel like this Ember Bluff place was a high point on this land.

The rational side of his brain yelled at him to run, but his conscience made him stay. *I owe Adam.*

"In here," Adam called as he vanished into the stable. What was waiting for Martin in there? He didn't want to think; he didn't deserve anything less than Adam's anger, and it would be so easy to walk away. It wasn't as if he had to stay here. It was only his fucked-up head that demanded he attempt to make amends. No sane man should walk into the gloomy darkness of the stable if he was being sensible.

Justin is right; you owe it to Adam for him to say his piece.

He clenched his fists, then relaxed them a finger at a

time, repeating the motion until the fluttering panic in his chest stilled. Then he held tightly to the rainbow quartz in his pocket. The crystal helped him focus, took him to a calmer place, and when he walked into the barn, he was mostly resigned to handling whatever happened next.

Adam was just inside, the cap pushed back, and Martin got his first look at the grown-up version of the boy he'd once known. The noises in the barn faded as he stared as if everything in his life so far had been leading up to this moment where he finally faced the second boy his father had hurt.

"I'm Adam." Adam held out his hand, and even though Martin's first instinct was to run, he took it without hesitation. Adam didn't shake it though. Instead he gripped Martin and pulled him closer, staring up close at him. There was a distinct lack of hatred or aggression in Adam's expression. In fact, it seemed he was searching deeply for something. Then he frowned and shook his head, evidently not having found what he was searching for. "I don't remember you," he said, sounding disappointed. Then he sighed and released his hold. "I thought you being there when something so intense happened, a memory that strong, might just be enough that I would remember it." He was rambling, then scrubbed at his eyes.

"Are you okay?" Martin asked on instinct. Adam seemed physically well, but his eyes had a distance to them.

He shook his head, then nodded. "Yeah, anyway, Justin says that you're the son of the man who locked us up and tried to kill us."

Christ, it couldn't get much blunter than that. What

could he say in response that would make any damn sense? "I want to say—"

"He also said that you were the one who left the doors open so we could get out, and that you advocated to keep us alive and in fact took some beatings for us and were a victim as much as we were."

Justin had said that?

"There wasn't anything else I could do. My dad—"

"No, don't talk about him or the others," Adam said. "I don't need to talk specifics."

"But—"

"No, it's best that way. Maybe the memories of them will come back to me one day, but right now, I don't want the details. I have the scars and what everyone has told me is enough to have me make sense of things, and that is all I want."

"If you're sure," Martin murmured, but all he could think was that he needed to be able to apologize and take the hits and make things halfway right.

"So, you negotiated to keep us alive and left the doors unlocked. You let us go. Right?"

"Yes, but—"

"Thank you," he said simply.

Martin cringed. "No, I was part of it. I didn't have much choice, but I could have done more. It's my fault—"

"So, do you know how to ride?" Adam interrupted with a warning look, taking the whole not-talking thing very seriously.

Martin wasn't following the change in direction of this conversation at all. "I've never ridden a horse."

"Well, you own a horse, and you need to learn how to ride. Let's go."

Own a horse? What did Adam mean?

"I don't understand."

"I'm going to teach you to ride. It's actually one of the things I never forgot. I guess because it's a muscle memory thing."

"Wait. No. Fuck." How could Adam be so calm? "How can you even look at me?"

Adam turned back to face Martin. "Jamie Crane right? I mean, that's your real name?"

"It is… was." He couldn't bear to use the name now. Just the sound of the syllables made him feel sick to the stomach.

"Well, I know we're not supposed to call you that in case people hear and track you back to your dad. That's right, isn't it?"

"I guess—"

"See, I have problems with my memory." Adam tapped his head. "Some things come back to me. Recently I've been recalling more, mostly about this dog I used to have when I was a kid. Scout his name was, some kind of collie cross. But some parts of it I'll never get back."

The guilt swallowed Martin whole. "Fuck—"

"I rely on the people around me, and Justin told me you were trapped as much as we were, that your father had a black soul, and that you didn't want to hurt us. So I trust Justin with my life. He's one of my best friends, and he's not the kind of person who would lie to me. Can you stand there and tell me he's lying about any of that?"

Martin shook his head. He had been trapped, abandoned by his mom, abused by Xander, forced to live a life that wasn't right, brainwashed through his respect for his dad. David Crane had the blackest soul of all men, and he'd locked his young son up when he was surplus to requirements. But no, Martin had never wanted to hurt anyone. That was the real truth in his heart; he'd just been desperate to survive.

"See, horses don't care about your past." Adam was changing the subject and stood next to a huge black-and-white horse. "They care about how you live in the present, about how you treat them, and what gifts you bring to them." He stroked the white mane, tangled his hands in the coarseness of it, and sighed. "I'm a lot like a horse, really, only flapjacks are my go-to snack, not apples," he said, then smiled. "This is Cookie, probably named because he's black and white, which makes him look like an Oreo, or at least that's what I think. He's new here, came to us with a bit of a past, via a rescue place, and he's yours."

"Sorry? What?" Martin decided he wasn't hearing right. Did Adam actually say that this big black beast of a horse was his? Since when did he own a horse? He'd never even owned a goldfish, let alone a big-ass horse.

"Everyone who lives and works here has a horse; yours is Cookie," Adam said with deliberate patience. "We think he's six or so now, docile, badly beaten down by previous owners, but still with a spark in him that we can gently encourage."

Was Adam talking about the horse or Martin himself?

"I'm not staying at Crooked Tree," Martin began but stopped when Adam threw him a glance and huffed a laugh.

"Yeah, you are. Now, let me talk you through this."

Martin didn't have space to argue, and he watched,

dazed, as Adam dressed the horse in all kinds of things. Or tacked up, which was the official term, and he really tried to concentrate. All he could think was that Adam had said he was staying and that somehow Justin and Adam didn't hate him as much as he deserved.

That was a blow. Something that rearranged his world order and left him unsettled and out of place.

They took it slow when they rode away from the stables, or at least Adam reassured Martin that the pace he set was slow, only his ass hitting the saddle didn't agree.

"Loosen your hold," Adam murmured, reining in his horse and helping Martin. "Imagine you had the bit in *your* mouth and someone was yanking on it, and you can begin to have empathy." There were several more adjustments, and by the time they made it to a large lake, he was actually managing to rise and fall with Cookie's movements, although he wasn't exactly enjoying the ride. There was a horse tied off already up here by a wide lake, and next to it was Justin, who'd clearly been waiting for them both.

He came straight over as Adam dismounted. "Okay?" he asked, the single word dripping with questions. *Are you okay? Did you talk to Martin? Do I have to kill him?*

"Fuck's sake, Justin, what are you doing up here?" Adam snapped. "Did Ethan tell you to come?"

Martin missed the answer, busy as he was trying to get off Cookie and nearly falling on his ass, but he could see Justin's shifty expression.

"He's just worried," Justin defended.

Adam sighed noisily. "I know. But I *can* do these things on my own, you know."

Justin shrugged, embarrassed, and Adam thumped him on the arm in a mock punch. Then the two bro-hugged, all backslapping and with linked hands, and something shifted inside Martin. When he'd left the doors unlocked, all those years ago, he'd prayed to any god that would listen to him that the two men be spared the fire, and seeing them here, grown and as friends, he felt as if that single prayer had been answered. If that was the only thing to come from his life, then he was happy. He noticed the huge boulder to one side, and it reminded him of the camp, and he climbed it and sat on the top, a view out over a beautiful lake, the mountains beyond. The last thing he wanted to do was get into any kind of heavy conversation with Justin and Adam right now.

"Catch." Justin tossed a bottle of water his way, and he caught it reflexively. Then he passed a water to Adam before holding his own aloft. "To not thinking about the past," he offered.

"Not being *able* to think about the past." Adam smirked. Then they looked expectantly at Martin.

What did they want him to say? His past was a horror, his future unsure, but what did the two of them need from him? He raised his water in salute; the words to match the gesture were harder to come by. Then it hit him that what made the best sense was to say what was in his heart.

"To you both," he murmured. And he meant it.

"So we've been talking," Justin said, clambering up to sit next to him. Adam followed, and took a seat on the other side so he was the meat in a Crooked Tree family sandwich.

"There's a job here if you want it," Adam said.

"Jay said you know your way around finances. Sam wants you to work with him."

"Sam?" Martin was dubious about Sam specifically wanting him.

Justin rolled his neck. "He said something about meatballs, and that was his reasoning. I didn't ask."

Adam joined in. "You could split your time: finance, Sam, working with the horses if you want, and we can set up a more permanent place for you to live. There's not a lot of money here, but it's a home."

"I'm not sure," Martin began.

"Give it a week," Justin said. "Then maybe another week after that. Nothing is stopping you from leaving, but right now, I can't see why you'd want to."

Tyler was one reason why. But the thought of living in a city, when there was so much sky here, so much peace, was appealing. Could they find a compromise for however long this affair lasted?

"A week," Martin agreed. "But I have something to do first. Could I have two days?" The money from his work with Tyler had arrived in his account, and there was enough to book a trip.

"Two days," Justin agreed. "But come back, and I promise I will tell you why I didn't kill you."

"I will." He shook hands with Justin and Adam, then they sat in companionable silence staring at the water. He wondered whether they were looking at the distant point where the mountain peak touched the sky or whether their view was nearer. One day he might know them well enough to ask them.

When he got back to the staff cabin with its shared space, he hid in his room and pulled out his cell to text Tyler the news, but he tried to write it and ended up backspacing so many versions that in the end he gave up. Tyler wanted him to go to Billings, to commute to Butte, maybe get a job, and that wasn't what he wanted to do. He didn't want a city or chaos or journeys in cars.

But he knew one thing he did want, and there was only one way to get it.

Chapter Nineteen

THE EARTHQUAKE STUDIES OFFICE ON THE MONTANA Tech campus was situated on the third floor of the Natural Resources Building, and even though he was fit, by the time Tyler reached his office, he was out of breath. This was due to the fact he'd hauled up the granodiorite he'd found at Crooked Tree, and with every step, it appeared to get heavier.

"Tyler, there's someone in reception for you," Jan called over. A fellow geologist, she noticed the granodiorite and came over to poke at it.

"Who is it?" He was expecting a package from North Carolina, statistical analysis paperwork they wanted him to examine.

"I didn't ask, sorry. Did you just carry this all the way up the stairs?"

He left her peering at the rock and chuckled under his breath. He recalled Martin carrying the rock down the hill to his cabin and the glare of indignation on his face at having to help. In hindsight, Tyler privately thought that was when he'd first started to fall for Martin.

He walked past the office where the data acquisition team worked and stopped to check on the thirty-sixth installation he'd just worked on. It was feeding back what was needed, showing a few peaking results, but nothing major. Part of him wished there was a problem because then he'd have the chance to go back to Crooked Tree to fix it, maybe take Martin with him, make love on a blanket under the stars.

I have it so bad.

He took the stairs two at a time, aware he must have just missed whoever was waiting for him, and they'd been there a while as he huffed and puffed up the stairs with the rock.

At first, he didn't see anyone, and then the receptionist pointed outside.

"He went outside, that way."

Suddenly he knew who was visiting, and he was breathless by the time he found Martin in the small park, sitting on a bench and staring upwards.

"Martin!" he said and sat next to him, waiting for him to turn so they could kiss. Martin didn't turn and maybe he wasn't here to kiss at all. Disappointment welled inside Tyler and took a tight hold.

"Hey," Martin murmured.

"Are you okay? What are you doing here?" Tyler asked.

"I don't know what I'm doing here," Martin turned to face him. "I guess I wanted to tell you that I'm staying at Crooked Tree for now, maybe for a long time, maybe so I can have a family. I don't know what I'm trying to say, but I know I can't live in a city, and I need Crooked

Tree right now. That doesn't mean I don't need you or that I don't love you, because I think I do. No, I know I do—"

Tyler stopped him talking with a kiss. When they parted, he smiled. "Banana."

They kissed again. The taste of Martin was intoxicating, and he wanted more.

"Can you say that again?" Tyler asked, cradling Martin's face in a familiar way.

"I love you."

"Good thing I love you, too. Also I have this plan. I'll get a permanent place near Crooked Tree and make it down there every spare moment I have. I don't have to spend every day in the office. I can take sabbaticals, remote research, installations, and you might be able to plan vacations to work with me when I'm surveying, and maybe we can start making a home together."

"You're serious?" Martin asked, his eyes wide with shock. "I thought I was coming here to explain… never mind."

"Explain why we can't be together? Nope, no way, not even entertaining that idea." He stood, inspired. "I'm taking my vacation. The agency owes me at least three weeks, I'll come back to Crooked Tree with you. We can find that place. We're only an hour away here, easy to commute, and maybe I can balance working remotely. You can start your new role, we can make love in our new bed and eat burned bacon, and we can take each day as it comes. What do you think?"

Martin didn't seem any less shocked, but this time it was tempered with a smile.

"Yes," he said simply.

And Tyler's world was changed by that single word.

MARTIN COULDN'T BELIEVE how long it took Tyler to work through the paperwork on his desk. The delay was half because he was meticulous about what piece of paper went where, but also that he reported to someone who was out of the office and had to wait for her to call in. With an agreement for a three-week work from home topographical analysis project in Tyler's pocket, they headed to Billings to pack some clothes for Tyler. Admitting he'd hitchhiked down to Butte had Tyler side-eyeing him, but at least it didn't mean they were bringing two cars back.

His apartment was spacious, and every window had a view of another building. Not grass or sky. Tyler didn't admit it, but he was relieved to get out. They headed north to Crooked Tree and drove straight through. It was mid-evening by the time they got there, and they parked Tyler's Prius between two SUVs.

"You know what?" Tyler began, his hands crossed on the wheel. "I never even checked to see if they have a free cabin here. My rental agreement on the other place is done and dusted."

"It was filled straight away. They're busy here. But you can stay with me in the staff cabin. I'm sure that will be okay. I hope it's okay. They said they were going to... never mind." They'd offered him a place of his own, but he didn't know what that meant. Maybe one of the more remote cabins? Or a tent somewhere? Who knew?

They got out of the car, carrying Tyler's bags, and for a moment Martin didn't know which way to go. Up to see Justin or Nate or one of the other people who would need to know he was back, or directly down to the staff cabin where maybe he and Tyler could take up where they'd left off with the kissing. They didn't get very far, caught by Sam on the bridge.

"Martin."

Martin still wasn't entirely sure about Sam's opinion of him. There had been that handshake before, but was this Sam waiting to warn Martin away?

"I have this for you." Sam held out his hand, and in his palm was a set of keys on a Crooked Tree keyring.

"What are those for?"

"Our place, or at least, it's your place now."

"Sorry?" Martin had begun to reach for the offered keys, but something stopped him. "What do you mean?"

"Justin and I always intended moving out. We have a place to go to: a new cabin in the woods, up behind the stables. You've probably seen it, a rambling thing with all these windows. If you're staying, and I think you should, you have your own place."

"I can't accept that."

Sam frowned. "Of course you can. Justin wants you to stay, Adam wants you to as well, and if Justin is happy…" He shrugged and then clapped a hand on Martin's shoulder. "Take it for what it is, dude, a place to start over with family. Don't let your brain fuck this up."

"But a whole place—"

"You'd be on-site; we were talking about you working with Jay, taking the finances off him, with Gabe teaching now. We'll all sit down and make decisions together. But, right now, go and see your place."

He and Tyler, who had hung back a little, shook hands, and then Sam extended his fist to Martin, who stared, confused. Sam reached out for his hand and formed it into a fist, then bumped the two together.

"We can talk more tomorrow."

Justin was standing a little way up and Martin drew back his shoulders and headed over to him.

"Thank you," he said, because that was the best and most perfect thing to say.

"I could have told you straight away when you first asked me why I didn't cross you off my list," Justin said, and pushed his hands deep in the pockets of his jeans. "I didn't because I wanted you to stay here, wanted to know what kind of man you'd become."

"Okay…"

"Love is why. When you asked me why I let you live, it was because of love. Because Sam showed me that my black and white world was actually filled with all different shades. I knew in my heart that you deserved something good in your life. So yeah," he looked down then and scuffed his foot in the mud. Martin had never seen him looking so vulnerable.

"Thank you for that," Martin said, and extended his hand to Justin. "Thank you for giving me the chance to find my own kind of love."

Justin smiled crookedly and took his hand, pulling him close in a brief bro-hug, and releasing him just as quickly.

"Now, go, look at your new place," Justin said, and stepped back and away, going down to join Sam. For a moment Martin stood still and alone, and then Tyler's arms came around his middle.

"Everything okay?" he asked, more than a little worry in his tone.

Martin tuned in Tyler's hold. "Everything is more than okay."

They headed up the stairs to the apartment, entering a big room with a small kitchen and two doors which he imagined were for the bedroom and bathroom. There was a huge basket on the counter, a card, and a balloon that said *New Home*, along with a bottle of champagne. He couldn't for one minute imagine that restrained-Justin had done this; it had to be Sam. He opened the card—a picture of a horse—and read the words out loud.

"We changed the sheets. Enjoy your new home. Sam and Justin."

Martin looked around again. It seemed to him they'd done a lot more than just changing sheets. The place was empty apart from a sofa. There were faded parts on the walls where photos had hung. They weren't returning.

This place was his. Tears pricked his eyes, and he ruthlessly pushed them away, but Tyler must have seen them because he pulled Martin into a hug and held him close.

"Tired?" Tyler asked when they moved apart. "Let's check out the bedroom."

Hand in hand they went into the bedroom, a large open space with a window and a tree close outside. The bed was certainly big enough for two men. On a small shelf, there was a glass vase filled with purple flowers, and next to it a plaque with the Crooked Tree logo, and inset into the O's were what looked like the gems he and Tyler had found at the creek. He traced the letters and couldn't help but smile as he saw his belongings had been moved here, piled neatly in the corner. It seemed he really had been evicted from the staff cabin. The room smelled of fabric conditioner, and the bed looked so inviting. He let out an unmanly squeak when Tyler jumped him and pushed him back onto the bed, rolling on his back and pulling Martin to sprawl over him.

"This could be your home," Tyler announced dramatically and kissed him. "You can make something here."

Something shifted inside Martin's heart, a cap of pain and self-hatred that he kept there to stop himself from hurting. What if he *did* stop here? What if he gave up trying to escape the past and maybe stopped to live in the present? With this place. With Justin and Adam, with Sam, and the rest of the characters who formed the family in this place. Not a toxic family that pretended to know how his life should be, but a group of people who just wanted him to try and be safe?

"I have a horse, you know," he announced to Tyler, who stopped kissing his neck to look him in the eye.

"A horse?"

"Cookie. His name is Cookie because he looks like an Oreo."

Tyler smiled into a kiss. "I love you, and for you, I'll learn to like horses." He kissed down Martin's body, divesting him of clothes, and then stripping his own, darting back into the main room and coming back with lube and condoms.

The vase rattled on the shelf, just enough to draw their attention.

"Earthquake," Tyler said. "Just a small one."

Martin tensed. "Earthquake? Shit. Maybe we should do something." Panic gripped him and he looked at the doorway. "Should we stand in a doorway?

Tyler chuckled. "That wasn't big enough to cause issues. It was just a small ground trembler."

"Yeah, but maybe you should just check the results. What if it gets worse?"

"I promise you, it was maybe a three, and I'm not leaving you right now for a regular non-happening. I want to stay right here, kissing you."

"You're sure?"

"If the ceiling falls on our head you can tell me I was wrong," Tyler deadpanned, and Martin stared right at him.

"What? You're joking. Right?"

Tyler kissed him then, "Of course I am. It would be the floor that would go first." He snorted a laugh and Martin pressed his lips together and tried to look serious.

"You're an asshole," he declared.

Tyler grinned then. "I promise it's nothing to worry about, now, less talking, more kissing."

The kisses grew so heated Martin was ready to come from rubbing against Tyler's thigh alone. Tyler pulled him on top in their usual position. Martin didn't *want* a usual position. He didn't want awkwardness and being careful, he wanted to experience fire and push his boundaries, and he wanted to feel at ease with Tyler.

"Make me feel it all," Martin murmured, and sat up, "fuck me."

"No, Martin, you don't need to—"

Martin kissed him quiet and then sat up and reached for the lube and slapped it into Tyler's hands. "I want you inside me, but you'll have to help me ride you."

Tyler's mouth fell open at his bold words, and for a few seconds he hesitated, looking uncertain, and it seemed Martin had to say something else.

"Please," he said. "I want to do it this way."

Tyler suited up, then squeezed lube onto his fingers, helping to ease the way, and when it was time, he helped and squirmed, and they laughed and smiled at the faintly ridiculous movements until there was no more laughing, and instead there was a sigh from Tyler and the impossible press and burn of Tyler's cock inside him. At first, it was unreal. It hurt, it pulled, it wasn't right, they weren't right, and Martin nearly climbed off and ran for the hills.

But then, in a smooth move, Tyler tilted his pelvis, pulled up his knee, and Martin's weight was supported and there…

"Fuck," Martin said, his balls tightening, his cock impossibly harder, and the sensations were incredible.

He pushed up, slid down, saw the tendons in Tyler's neck as he gritted his teeth and tilted his head back. "So close," Tyler groaned, and then he closed his hand around Martin's cock, and the end was quick. Just the touch of his hand, Tyler's cock in his ass, he felt impossibly full and tight, and he held on to his orgasm as long as he could until there was no holding it back. He shot hard, painting Tyler's chest, as Tyler heaved up and cursed as he came as well.

Martin slumped then, carefully lying on Tyler, sticky, messy, and utterly sated. He could be happy here; he could have this.

"This is home," he whispered against Tyler's throat. "Here in this place, but mostly here with you."

But Tyler was asleep, and Martin couldn't move, and he gave in to the inevitable and slept.

. . .

WHEN HE AWOKE the next morning, scratchy, aching in all the right places, he knew one thing for sure. He'd not had a single nightmare.

"Morning sunshine," Tyler called cheerfully from the door. "Bacon's nearly done. Grab a shower."

Martin showered, shaved, and rummaged in his bags for clean jeans of which he had one pair left. Then he borrowed one of Tyler's sweatshirts emblazoned with the logo *Geology Rocks*, and ambled out to the scent of slightly charred bacon.

"Look at you in your boyfriend's stuff," Tyler teased as they kissed good morning, and then they sat at the small breakfast bar to eat. A knock interrupted them a few moments in, but it was Tyler up off his seat and heading down the stairs to the door with encouragement that Martin eat faster because they had things to do. Martin didn't want to know what those things were. He was more focused on starting his new career here at Crooked Tree doing whatever they thought he could do.

Finance probably. He was good with numbers. His skills in the kitchen were limited, but he was a quick learner, and mostly he was good with the guests. They liked him. He could do that.

He heard Tyler's footsteps on the stairs with those of a second person, and Tyler looked around the room quickly, already ridiculously house-proud. Then he stood to face whoever was visiting. It would probably be Justin or Sam again or maybe Jay wanting to talk finance.

He pasted a smile on his face, feeling calm, feeling centered, and then he saw who was with Tyler.

His sister. Alice.

"There's someone here for you," Tyler said a little late and moved aside.

She stood there, uncertain, her long wavy hair a cloak around her shoulders, and she didn't move toward him.

"You shouldn't be here," Martin said, loud enough for her to hear.

"Jamie," she murmured when she was near enough that they could talk without shouting. Right behind her, Tyler didn't move, but his presence was welcome and reassuring.

"Martin," he corrected her. "I'm not Jamie anymore."

"Martin, I'm sorry—"

Fear gripped him, and he wanted to push her away, then slam the door shut and lock himself inside. "You shouldn't be here. I promised your stepfather I wouldn't talk to you."

"I know what he said," she said, and a single tear rolled down her face. "But I want to know my brother."

"There's not much to know," Martin said, and now he was defensive. "Our mom vanished with you and left with me with a psychopath."

She winced, and he felt all the guilt. She hadn't even been born, so technically Mom hadn't *taken* her instead of him.

"I know she did. But, when she found out she was dying she told me about her brilliant boy. Look, can we talk, alone…" She indicated Tyler, who immediately took a step to leave.

"No, Tyler stays. Whatever happens here, Tyler can be here with me. Please don't make him leave." Oh god, he sounded pathetic, broken, and an overwhelming blackness threatened to consume him.

"Mom had to leave. He was going to kill her." Alice

didn't wait to leap into defending their mom. "Then, she met my stepdad in the hospital. He was a politician, there for… look, it doesn't matter… all you have to understand is that she jumped from the frying pan into the fire. He controlled her as much as David Crane did but it was a lot more subtle."

She paused, and he could see the tears in her eyes, wondered at the kind of life she'd had.

"I loved Mom," she continued. "And I'll never forgive her that she didn't tell me about you until it was too late. But, please don't hate her, and don't hate me. You're my big brother, and I want you in my life."

She held out a hand imploringly, and when he didn't immediately take it, she turned to leave. "okay," she murmured.

Only, out of everything she'd said, there was only one thing he'd really heard, and he caught up with her at the door a few strides away. "I couldn't ever hate you," he reassured immediately.

She turned to face him, and there was hope on her face.

"You're my little sister, and…"

"I know you came to Mom's funeral. Dad told me when I confronted him about you."

"You confronted your dad?"

"Mom told me he knew about you, that she asked for his help to find you. The excuses were all there. You moved too much. You didn't have a fixed address. Then he told her our dad had died and that the trail had gone cold." She was so earnest, so open, and his cloak of fear began to fade.

"It's okay," he said offhand.

She shook her head. "Please, Ja—Martin, you're all I

have left, and I need to… I want to…" Tears ran down her face, and she held out a hand again. This time he took her hand and held her.

"Hello, Martin," she said.

"Hello, Alice," he replied.

They talked for the longest time, Tyler heading out at one point to bring back food. By the time Alice fell asleep on the sofa, wrapped in a thick blanket, Martin was exhausted as well, crawling into his bed and snuggling back into Tyler.

He had a home, a sister, and a man he loved.

How did he get to be so lucky?

Epilogue

TWO YEARS LATER

"Are you ready, Martin?"

Alice paced the room, they were already five minutes late, and one thing he'd learned about his feisty sister was that she hated to be late.

"I can't do this... thing."

She tutted and crossed to him, helping him with the burgundy tie. It matched the color of her dress, and she had it tied properly in a few seconds.

"There." She patted his chest and smoothed his jacket. "You look so handsome." She sounded choked, and he pulled her in for a hug. They'd traveled a hard road these last two years, both of them fighting their own ghosts, but here, today, they were as good as they'd ever been.

"And you look beautiful," he murmured in her ear. The word had long since lost its power to evoke awful memories. All he had to do was recall the tone of the word when Tyler whispered it to him and he felt a warmth that stayed with him for hours.

"Okay, big brother, let's go."

A moment of doubt hit him as he stepped outside. What he was doing today was a miracle, a dream that he never thought would ever happen. He loved Tyler, and Tyler loved him, and at Christmas when Tyler had gone down on one knee and proposed, he'd said yes in an instant. There had been not one millisecond of hesitation. He held the rainbow crystal tight, and focused on what he wanted.

He wanted Tyler. He wanted forever. To him, the two things were the same.

Their honeymoon was planned, the Jeep already packed. Two weeks in the tents by the stream, with a double cot, looking for sapphires and maybe a fleck or two of gold. Perfect.

Tyler was there already, standing under an arch of flowers, his family behind him. Then, hand in hand with Alice, Martin headed to join his fiancé.

"Hey, beautiful," Tyler whispered.

"Hey back."

Alice squeezed his hand and then made a show of passing her hold to Tyler's.

Martin turned and faced Tyler and repeated their vows. Tyler never let go of him, and Martin gripped tight. They exchanged rings of Montana gold, and inset into each were the six tiny gemstones they'd found in the creek, taken from the picture frame, with three in each ring; a link to the time they met, and an anchor to the place they called home.

"I love you," he said as they were finally told they could kiss.

Tyler cradled his cheek with his free hand, and Martin was lost in his hazel eyes, and then he smiled.

He couldn't believe how far he'd come. From being a kid broken through violence and fire to finding this man with his sapphires and his rambling and his warm welcoming heart. The future for them was bright, and he finally had an extended family that made sense. How had he gotten so lucky to have found Crooked Tree and Tyler?

Really he had only one thing to say to the man who'd stolen his heart.

"I love you too."

THE END

Also by RJ Scott

The Texas Series

The Heart Of Texas, Texas Book 1

Riley Hayes, the playboy of the Hayes family, is a young man who seems to have it all: money, a career he loves, and his pick of beautiful women. His father, CEO of HayesOil, passes control of the corporation to his two sons; but a stipulation is attached to Riley's portion. Concerned about Riley's lack of maturity, his father requires that Riley *'marry and stay married for one year to someone he loves'*.

Angered by the requirement, Riley seeks a means of bypassing his father's stipulation. Blackmailing Jack Campbell into marrying him "for love" suits Riley's purpose. There is no mention in his father's documents that the marriage had to be with a woman and Jack Campbell is the son of Riley Senior's arch rival. Win/win.

Riley marries Jack and abruptly his entire world is turned inside out. Riley hadn't counted on the fact that Jack Campbell, quiet and unassuming rancher, is a force of nature in his own right.

This is a story of murder, deceit, the struggle for power, lust and love, the sprawling life of a rancher and the whirlwind existence of a playboy. But under and through it all, as Riley learns over the months, this is a tale about family and everything that that word means.

Complete Series

The Heart Of Texas

Texas Winter

Texas Heat

Texas Family

Texas Christmas

Texas Fall

Texas Wedding

Texas Gift

Home For Christmas

RJ Scott - have you read?

Bodyguards Inc series

A mix of family, friends, danger and sexy bodyguards.

- Book 1 – Bodyguard to a Sex God
- Book 2 – The Ex Factor
- Book 3 – Max and the Prince
- Book 4 – Undercover Lovers
- Book 5 – Love's Design
- Book 6 – Kissing Alex

The Heroes series

A series of three books featuring a SEAL, a Marine and a Cop, and the guys that fall for them…

- A Reason To Stay - Book 1
- Last Marine Standing - Book 2
- Deacons Law - Book 3

Texas series

Cowboys, a ranch, family, and love.

Connect with RJ Scott

RJ is the author of the over one hundred and thirty published novels and discovered romance in books at a very young age. She realized that if there wasn't romance on the page, she could create it in her head, and is a lifelong writer.

She lives and works out of her home in the beautiful English countryside, spends her spare time reading, watching films, and enjoying time with her family.

The last time she had a week's break from writing she didn't like it one little bit, and has yet to meet a bottle of wine she couldn't defeat.

www.rjscott.co.uk | rj@rjscott.co.uk

NEWSLETTER

facebook.com/author.rjscott

twitter.com/Rjscott_author

instagram.com/rjscott_author

bookbub.com/authors/rj-scott

pinterest.com/rjscottauthor